the Edumacation of Jay Baker

the Edumacation of Jay Baker

JAY CLARK

Christy Ottaviano Books
Henry Holt and Company
New York

Henry Holt and Company, LLC
Publishers since 1866
175 Fifth Avenue
New York, New York 10010
macteenbooks.com

Library of Congress Cataloging-in-Publication Data
Clark, Jay.
The edumacation of Jay Baker / Jay Clark.—1st ed.
p. cm.
Summary: In small-town Ohio, fifteen-year-old Jay Baker's popular new blog helps him navigate high school as he faces off against his mortal enemy, meets the girl of his dreams, and watches his parents' relationship implode.
ISBN 978-0-8050-9256-1 (hc)
[1. High schools—Fiction. 2. Schools—Fiction. 3. Family problems—Fiction. 4. Best friends—Fiction. 5. Friendship—Fiction. 6. Blogs—Fiction.] I. Title.
PZ7.C553553Edu 2012 [Fic]—dc23 2011025590

First Edition—2011 / Designed by Patrick Collins
Printed in the United States of America by R.R. Donnelley & Sons Company, Harrisonburg, Virginia

1 3 5 7 9 10 8 6 4 2

To Dad—

for playing the steadfast melody to my unchained harmony.

To Mom—

for always believing I could go my own way.

To Ann—

for turning a house into a home.

To Amy—

for being the wind beneath my Whoopee cushion.

To Caroline—

for putting a lot more heavenly in my day.

I love you all.

The Tracks in My Ears

the Edumacation of Jay Baker

DISC ONE
BUSTED RHYMES (FEATURING GAY BAKER)

TRACK 1

Don't You Remember You Told Me You'd Feed Me Pizza?

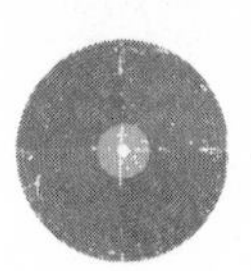

Mom and Dad were in their room with the door shut. Again. Cautiously, I pressed my ear against the wooden frame. Hakuna Matata, no Discovery Channel–like sounds could be heard. Only two mammals speaking so quickly and intensely that their voices were nearly inaudible.

Mom: "You're never home enough to know how . . . ta garba gunkin gooble gariation."

Dad: "Where were you when . . . aveno espresso somato Arantxa Sánchez Vicario?"

Huh? Just when it seemed I'd get the gist of the conversation, they'd start mumbling in a language known only to the Sims.

An odd noise rang out, causing me to jump back from the door.

Turned out to be my stomach growling for the pizza Mom and Dad had promised earlier. I was hesitant to interrupt them for funding, though, and my recent birthday present to myself—a MacBook Pro, fifteen years in the making—had left me cash poor. One last payment option: my body. I doubted Amore's Pizzeria would barter a slice of this for one of theirs.

I walked back downstairs, grabbed my cell from my room, and called my best friend, the satirically named Cameo Appearance Parnell (thanks to her cuckoo mother).

"Cameo Appearance Parnell speaking." She answered professionally, knowing it was me from the caller ID on her cell.

"Yes, is Cameo Parnell there, please?" I asked, equally professional.

"Yes, she's speaking and stuff."

"But is she there, ma'am?"

"Depends. Who's calling?"

"Me. What are you doing, fool?"

"I kissed a girl . . . and . . . I . . . liiiiked iiiit," she sang slowly, painfully, like the Katy Perry Auto-Tune was a ballad. "Something something, can't remember the wooords, cheeerry ChapStick."

There was only one question to ask.

"Why?"

"Just testing out an emotional reinterpretation for my *American Idol* audition," she explained. "I'm making it my own."

"It sounds like you're making out with it."

"Even better."

Cameo was actually a great singer, and her ultimate goal was to execute a Kelly Clarkson breakaway from our hometown of Indian Lake, Ohio. Home of . . . the great man-made

Indian Lake, three "dollar stores" (one Family Dollar, two Dollar Generals), McDonald's, and Low Bob's Tobacco, a drive-thru tobacco outlet located in an abandoned Kentucky Fried Chicken building. My parents, cigarette enthusiasts till their last drag of breath, were loyal customers.

"Hate to break it to you gently again, Cam, but you're fifteen and ineligible to try out until next year."

"All the more reason to get a jump-start on the competish. Speaking of which, have you started practicing for next Monday's big debate yet?"

"I don't wanna talk about it."

Let the record show that I'd signed up to run for class president without knowing about the First Anal Freshman Class Presidential Debate—a last-minute addition by our overenthusiastic government teacher, Ms. Lambert.

"I can't believe you're running," Cameo said.

"Me either."

"Remind me of the reason again?"

Yep, Cameo was the (wrong) reason. A snizzly little cheerleading dynamo with long blond hair and a Kate-Hudson-cum-jailbait face—I'd loved her now for many moons. But she gravitated toward jocks like her on-again, off-again boyfriend, Wade Pierson, not nerds with straight-A report cards. I caught Luigi on my Mario Kart, not balls. But if I grew a pair and became class president, well, maybe I'd morph into a candidate worthy of Cam. The plan was total shit.

"Next topic."

"I broke up with Wade," she said.

Off-again.

"Nice," I said. "When did you realize he was a tool of Seacrestian proportions?"

"When his hands tried to measure *my* proportions."

"Unfortunate."

"Yeah, I thought he was the one," she said sarcastically.

"At least you maintained custody of your dignity," I said.

"Exactly. Now, where was I?"

She resumed singing "I Kissed a Girl" before I could protest.

After Cameo and I hung up, I plopped down at my desk, opened my MacBook, and began typing notes on our latest conversation into my journal. I'd named my sleek new toy Alba, in honor of renowned thespian Jessica, and she really understood where I was coming from on a variety of sexually frustrated levels.

Twenty minutes passed until my stomach growled again. Over it, I trotted back up the stairs and rapped on my parents' door, calling out, "Mom? Dad?"

"Come in, Buckwheat," Dad said.

I entered.

They were seated on the bed, Mom on her side and Dad on his, a whole lotta Weird Al in between them.

"Hey, Buckwheat," Mom said, choking on the words.

Buckwheat was their nickname nod to my uncontrollably messy hair (minus the politically incorrect undertones). For the longest time I'd thought Mom and Dad were saying "Buttwheat," which had baffled me. *Wheat comes from the butt?* Google.com.

"Can I order the pizza from Amore's yet?" I asked.

My parents' room was huge and dimly lit—"mood lighting" as Mom had put it one time after one too many brewskies—so at first I couldn't see their faces. However, as I stepped closer to their gargantuan four-poster bed, I realized that Mom's cheeks were flushed and splotchy from crying.

My eyes searched hers for an explanation, but the look she gave me in response said she wasn't ready to provide one.

I turned to Dad. He appeared to be shaken, too, but was covering better. Quickly, he unfurled some bills from his money clip and told me to get pepperoni on half for my seventeen-year-old sister, Abby, who was holed up in her room as usual, in between friends' houses and/or trips to her boyfriend Eric's nether regions.

"We have to make sure she eats so she can keep up her texting strength," he said in a halfhearted attempt at humor.

"Don't forget updating her Facebook page," I added. "Eight thirty-five p.m. Abby Baker . . . is analyzing the sociocultural ramifications of the Jessica Simpson Mom Jeans Scandal. Maybe I should ghostwrite that one for her, Mom?"

A merchant at The Limited HQ in Columbus before schlepping to suburbia to raise a family, Mom was as close to a fashionista as one could come by in Ohio.

"Sure," Mom said. "That leopard-print belt . . ." But she trailed off, unable to complete her critique.

"Okay," I said, stepping backward. "I'll get right on that."

What was going on up in here was definitely not *amore*.

TRACK 2

What's Vicky's Secret Got to Do with It?

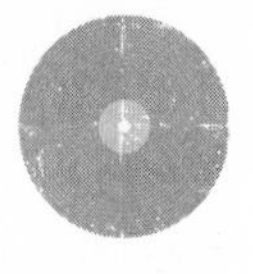

"Do you think they're getting a D-bomb?" Cameo asked me quietly at lunch the next day.

We were sitting beside each other at a round table full of our assorted friends: Jennifer, the modern-day flower child and pot enthusiast; her loyal boyfriend and green-thumbed provider, Greg; Cameo's space-cadet sidekick, Sangria (for real). Directly across from us sat a pretty new girl who'd hitched her shy little wagon to our olly-olly-oxen, Caroline—heavy into tennis and not much interested in talking to anything other than the strings of her racket on the school's courts.

As usual, Cameo and I were focused on each other.

"I have no idea," I said through a mouthful of fries. "They don't fight in front of me."

"Key words, *in front of you*," Cameo said. "My parents are the exact opposite, as you know. Last night during dinner, Dad was so frustrated with Mom that he threw a plate and almost hit her cat."

"Not Mittens Parnell . . ."

Cam drank deeply from her Yoo-hoo bottle. "It was a paper plate. And it kind of fluttered anticlimactically. Is that a word? The point is, he did it in front of me after Mom said something nasty about him scheduling eight million chiropractor appointments when he never does anything. Your parents are fighting behind closed doors because they're hiding something. We should make like a *Scooby-Doo!* episode and investigate."

She ran her hands roughly through my shaggy bedhead, and the follicles stood on end, begging for more stimulation.

"Not today, *Velma*," I said, deliberately choosing the frumpy asexual sleuth over the delectable Daphne to irritate her. "I have too much on my paper plate with this freaking debate. Ms. Lambert gave us a list of questions during government today, and they all suck."

At the bottom of the list, she'd added helpfully, "Don't choke, my little chicken nuggets. And please don't start feeling sorry for yourselves because I'm making you take a crash (and burn?) course in public speaking. This debate will put feathers on your chests. Mwahahaha. XOXO—Gossip Girl."

I snuck a glance over at my opponent, Mike "the Herp" Hibbard, the fat-ass yang to my flat-ass yin, holding court amongst a plethora of freshman d-bags whose personalities reeked almost as much as his did. Formerly friends, Mike and I stopped being cool in seventh grade when sports became school-related. I quit them all, and he took a fancy to calling me gay on a regular basis (still did). Rather than figure out the impetus behind his sudden hatred of all things Gay Baker, one day I snuck into health class before the bell rang, posted an unflattering picture of him on the dry-erase board, and wrote underneath it, "Morbid Obesity: Exhibit A." It was a big hit, so I decided to cook up a series—"Some Pig," inspired by *Charlotte's Web*, being a real highlight—and promptly lost all my guy friends. The athletes followed Mike.

"Is Jay there?" Cameo asked.

"Jay's brain is out to lunch right now. Can I take a message?"

"Mm-hmm, can you ask it to pick me up a five-dollar footlong?"

"Actually," I said, needing a breather, "I'm gonna go get some fruit snacks. You want anything?"

"Another spot of Yoo-hoo for the lady!" she cried as I got up from my seat.

I walked over to the kitcheteria, grabbed our respective sugar fixes, and took my place in the cashier's line.

From behind me, a familiar voice said, "I saw you go straight for the fruit snacks, ya fruit. You're so open about your gayness these days."

The hairs on the back of my neck prickled, but this time not in a good way. I turned around to find Mike Hibbard's beady eyes narrowing into dim-witted slits.

"They can only stock so much food in the cafeteria for you and your baby, Mike. Give people in next period's lunch the opportunity to eat."

Standing six feet tall, Mike was my height with fifty pounds extra in the gut region. He squeezed his fists in an apparent effort to intimidate me, and the king-size Rice Krispies Treat in his hand slipped out.

"Just like on the football field," I said, laughing as he bent down to retrieve it.

"You won't be laughing during the debate Monday, Gay. Since Ms. Lambert gave us that cheat sheet, I know exactly how I'm going to humiliate you in front of Cameo and everyone else."

Mike's mention of Cameo and the debate unnerved me, and I couldn't think of a witty reply.

So I went with an old standby: "Yeah, but I'll always have your mom to comfort me."

Mike was a momma's boy, even more so than me, and like clockwork his cheeks turned bright red. He lurched forward and attempted to grab the collar of my Lacoste-a-lot shirt, but then the line cleared, and I was in plain sight of the cashier before he could get a grip.

"I'm paying for the Rice Krispies Treat behind me, too," I said to the cashier, handing her exact change. "Just doing my part to support teen pregnancy."

The woman gaped at me, confused, and I walked away without looking back at the expectant mother f'er—more nervous about the debate than ever.

"Are we investigating at your house tonight or what?" Cameo asked upon my return. She hadn't noticed the run-in with Mike.

"I'm powerless to stop you," I said, figuring I should enjoy her company while I still could.

"Right," she said, "I'm a Tour de France."

"Tour de force."

"Yes, that too."

She ran her fingers through her hair, her blue eyes suddenly serious. "Jay?"

"Yeah?"

"I really do hope everything is okay between your mom and dad."

"Thanks. Me too."

Cameo rode the bus to my home on Horseshoe Channel Drive without clearing it with her whackjob parents. They didn't care. Nor did mine, though. I wasn't perceived as a baby-making threat by anyone, apparently, which was understandable. Even with my braces finally off and my eyes the cerulean blue of my beautiful Aryan mother's, I wasn't exactly oozing sex appeal through my third-world body. Just occasionally stuff from my face.

We walked in and headed straight for Mom and Dad's bedroom to kick off our search party (without a bang, unfortunately). Guilt, guilt, guilt pounded inside my chest as I turned the knob and opened the door. Couldn't help it; being in my parents' room when they weren't around made me feel like a featured perv on *To Catch a Predator.*

Cameo had no such reservations. She boldly made her way to their dresser and began methodically sifting through my mother's tapestry of loincloths like it was just another day at the mall.

"Do you really think my mom is stupid enough to hide

incriminating evidence underneath something that says Victoria's Secret? Granted, she's no stranger to the bleach cap, but she has her bachelor's—give the lady a few semesters' worth of credit."

"Here's my theory: your dad sells more insurance than twenty Geico cavemen combined, so money can't be the issue here. Mommy or Daddy Baker must be seeking a little sexual healing, afternoon delight, bon voy-boinkage from another party. And people get careless when performing their random acts of in-dis-cre-tion."

"Where did you learn that word?" I asked, trying my best to avert her I'm-so-right-about-this look. "Have you been DVR'ing crap on the E! Channel again?"

"Of course," she said, holding up a pair of Dad's Jockeys, to my dismay.

"Jeez, Cam, you're practically a Kardashian."

"Thanks!"

Of course she took that as a compliment.

Finished rummaging through my parents' drawers, Cam skipped over to their massive walk-in closet.

"Good luck finding anything in there," I said, following behind obediently.

"Must you provide a running negative commentary?" she asked.

"It's my gift from Baby Jesus."

"I just prayed that he'd take it back."

"Take that back."

"No."

The closet contained boxes upon boxes of "memories"

that pack-rat Mom was reluctant to throw out. Cameo tore through them with vigor, uncovering Mom's dusty record collection, musty Halloween costumes, and fussy decorations that had once adorned the thrift store Mom helped her septuagenarian friend, Celia Cowell, manage. Whereabouts Town brought the masses Maude-like muumuus and Karen Carpenter pantsuits since 1972, despite Mom's best attempts to freshen up the inventory.

I was thinking something to the effect of "if only Cam would shower some of this attention to detail on me, then maybe we could take a shower together," when she lifted a folded piece of paper from the bottom of Mom's auxiliary jewelry box, a huge smile on her freckle-dusted face.

She wrinkled her little snub nose, and with arms outstretched cried, "Jinkies!"

Then she unfolded the paper. "Yo Gabba Gabba . . . I think it's a love letter."

Mom's love doctor had written her a prescription for five hundred milligrams of sexy time. Had she filled it? Mental picture, mental picture.

I grabbed the letter from Cameo's hand and started reading it aloud.

TRACK 3

Love Fax, Never Meant to See

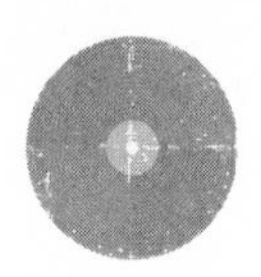

Mom's secret love note turned out to be from my least probable suspect: Dad. True to form, he'd written it on a fax cover sheet.

Hey, Big Mama—
Big Dad, kiddies' pal, here. Just wanted you to know that I still love everything about you. The way you throw your head back when you laugh, the way your brow furrows when you're deciphering our online bank statement, the way you are with our kids—all of it. I'm still so proud that you're my wife. I know I've been working a lot lately, and sometimes when I come home all I want to do is

*eat my beans and wienies and watch M*A*S*H. Just know that I'm putting in these long hours for us, because you deserve the best in life. Bear with me for a little longer, and remember this note when you're lonely at night and waiting for me to come home. Things will get better soon, promise.*

Happy Nineteenth Anniversary,
Big Dad

"When was their nineteenth?" Cam asked when she'd finished reading it again.

"A month ago," I replied somberly.

"Sounds like your mom hasn't been getting any McLovin' for a while. Ba-da-bah-bah-baaaaaah . . . too soon for jokes, isn't it?"

"Yep."

"I'm really sorry, Jay," she said sympathetically. "This whole thing is so . . . sad. I can't imagine what you must be feeling. Well, I kind of can, considering the parental-coaster I've been riding the past fifteen years, but I always thought yours were different."

"Yeah, well, sorry to disappoint you."

I just sat there, simmering on the floor uselessly, while Cameo put the closet back in order. She kept asking if I was okay, but I was in *Another World* hoping *The Cosby Show* would come back on, trying to remember the last time I'd seen my parents exhibit a Cliff & Clair Huxtable level of camaraderie—not counting the Hawkeye-assisted laughs they shared while sitting on the couch watching TV. ("Not funny," I'd call out from the bar while doing my homework.) They never went out to dinner anymore. They used to go hot-tubbing together, but I couldn't recall the last time I'd been grossed out by the sight of them in their bathing suits, dancing and wiggling their backsides for my benefit.

And when had I last seen them kiss? Heard them coo "kissy-kissy!" when I unwittingly caught them in the act, usually in the laundry room folding clothes. Mom: "Your dad was just being my special helper." Me: "Is that what you kids are calling it these days?"

This Love Fax could kiss it, suck it, twist it, pull it, bop it, ad nauseam. I placed it back inside Mom's jewelry tomb and tried to forget about its apocalyptic existence.

My denial worked well for a day.

The next night, while Mom put in some extra hours at Whereabouts Town for inventory rollover ("a *turnover* would require selling some merchandise," she'd joked good-naturedly), Dad, Abby, and I were eating dinner at the kitchen bar when he announced a family meeting. It was set for Friday: a last-minute nightmare for Abby because she was dying to go to Harold's Haunted Cornfield with her friends, code for "let's go to someone's parent-free house and get wasted." Unsurprisingly, Friday wasn't a problem for me. I needed to catch up with Alba MacBook, but otherwise had no plans outside the home.

"Why does it have to be on a Friday night, Daaaad?" Abby whined. "I'm not sure when I'll be able to go again."

"Go on Saturday," Dad said, one eye on the Reds game.

"I'm sure your windup-toy followers will still be available," I added helpfully, clapping my hands together as I thought one of her monkeys would.

"There's a football scrimmage on Saturday, dumb ahh-pple," she said, throwing a touchdown of a dirty look my way. "You'd know that if you weren't so insistent on remaining socially and athletically inept."

This wasn't offensive. Abby had a way of ragging on me that just wasn't. She was my sister; she loved me in spite of her menstrual cycle, and I was the only person besides Dad whom she couldn't shut out entirely.

"I resent the 'athletically,'" I said. "My Wii dexterity is better than ever."

"Which reminds me, I really wish you'd quit taking so long in the shower," she said, gesturing lewdly.

We both threw our heads back and laughed—the sound the same cadence as our mother's.

"Real nice, Abby," Dad said. "If we get through the meeting in time, you can still scream to your heart's content at the cornfield. And that's all I have to say 'bout that."

Ah, the inevitable *Forrest Gump* quote. Run, Forrest, run, before he quotes you again.

"Yes, Jen-ny," I said to Abby, "I'm sure the meeting will fly by like a bird."

I stifled a laugh—Dad was a notoriously slow and

deliberate talker. Abby knew this and threw a Tater Tot in my direction. I ducked, unnecessarily, and it landed in my lap. My Ore-Ida retaliation almost made me forget that our home life really was like a big box of questionable-looking chocolates right now.

TRACK 4

WII WILL ROCK YOU AT THE FAMILY MEETING

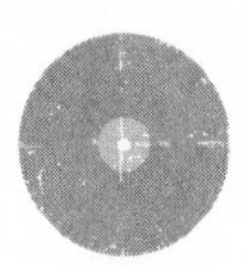

Friday night. Family meeting. It all happened so fast. Mom and Dad were nervous Nellies, horses foaming at the mouth and feeding off each other's skittish energy. There was no time-delayed lecturing from Dad, after all—only rapid-fire promises and reassurances.

My sister and I were sitting at the bar; Mom and Dad were in the kitchen, awkwardly attempting to present a united front.

"Your mom and I have decided to separate for a bit," Dad said.

"Nothing has been set in stone," Mom said.

"No, nothing is definite," Dad said. "We're going to try it."

"We're not getting a divorce," Mom said. "This doesn't necessarily mean anything. Nothing is changing for you guys."

"No, nothing will change," Dad confirmed. "You'll still live here. Your mom is going to move out for a few months. For now."

"I'm only moving down the road," Mom said. "Holiday Shores."

The nearby trailer park that was no one's idea of a holiday.

"It's a nice trailer," she added quickly, probably because of my facial expression. "It's close by, and since this may only be temporary, your dad and I didn't want to rent anything too expensive. It won't be so bad. I've already picked out new furniture. A new TV. A plasma, Jay. You can bring your Wii over. It will be okay."

"Things are going to be okay," Dad repeated.

He looked down and shuffled his "boat shoes," the pair of brown leather loafers he insisted on wearing with white tube socks. (I always teased him that there was some kind of childhood issue there.) Then his milky brown eyes searched Abby's, a pair just like his. Then mine, just like Mom's.

"Do you guys have any questions?"

Yeah, I thought angrily, I can think of a few thousand.

I jumped off the bar stool and headed toward Mom's fully-stocked Longaberger candy basket at the end of the counter, stepping over the immobile body of Buffy Baker, our highly unmotivated golden retriever. I grabbed a bag of Sour Patch Kids (SPKs); tried to look engrossed in my search for the red dye #40 species, but another tremor of anger shot up my spine.

I kneeled down to pet Buffy and examine Mom and Dad from a new vantage point. They were both attractive in a parental-figure kind of way: With her reasonably rockin' body, including a pair of legs Dad said "would make Tina Turner hit the treadmill," Mom was still considered a blond bombshell in her mid-forties. Although she often chose outfits that showcased her gams, like the African safari dress she had on now, she kept the hemlines Katie Couric classy. Aside from his nighttime boat shoes, Dad was still working the distinguished Brooks Brothers businessman look to perfection during the day. His full head of salt-and-pepper hair just might appeal to an ambitious secretary looking to climb the corporate ladder. They both looked guilty to me in that moment.

Traitors. Who was cheating on whom? The Love Fax pointed to Mom. . . .

The problem with the prolonged silence that resulted from my hyperactive speculation was that Abby certainly wasn't going to fill the verbal void. The girl was definitely an island, and good luck to anyone rowing ashore, even while she wasn't looking. She'd pick up their scent from on high, grab their paddle, and beat them down with it. LOST.

Since childhood, Abby had held her feelings inward. "Emotionally constipated, like me" was how Dad fondly referred to her condition. "Even when she was in diapers, she didn't want to hug me," Mom would say, shrugging her shoulders and frowning in that guilt-inducing way that only mothers could. Abby was impervious to that disappointed look; I wasn't. When Mom found herself wondering why her relationship with Abby remained so distant, I was the child who bridged the gap and gave up a hug or three to placate her.

"Are you guys okay?" Dad asked, waking me from my reverie.

Avoiding the question, I was about to raid the refrigerator when out of the corner of my eye I noticed two tears streaming down Abby's face. Only two. She didn't wipe them off; that would only serve to draw attention to the act. My tough-as-nails sister was crying, and that shook my foundation to the core. Made me realize that this disaster was real and seismic and not going anywhere.

"I think we need some time to absorb the shock, Dad," I said. "Can we talk more tomorrow?"

Dad glanced at Abby, caught on like he usually did, and agreed.

And that was it. Our family was done. Everyone scattered. Dad headed for the TV, Mom started wiping down the kitchen counter, Abby went to her room, and I just sat there twisting back and forth on the bar stool, wondering what to do next.

TRACK 5

YOU AIN'T NOTHING BUT A HOOCHIE MAMA, I GUESS

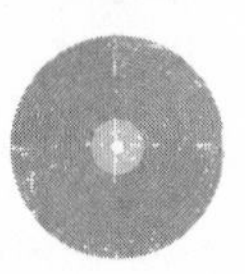

Lying underneath the covers of my bed, hours later, I was drowning in deep thought. No cogent explanations bubbled to the surface. Nothing made sense.

Earlier, my parents had separately stopped by my room on their way up to bed: Mom to be sure I was warm enough (the woman slept with four heavy blankets and a sentimentally overvalued Technicolor dream robe on top for good measure—Mt. Mommy, as I'd called it when I was little), Dad to provide his juvenile yet scientifically accurate "don't let the bedbugs bite" warning. Basically, they'd treated me with kid gloves, and I'd returned the favor by not demanding to know what was going on.

I looked over at the Larry Bird poster Dad had given me in the first grade, hanging on my closet door. Both former premier high school athletes, Dad and Mom had tried everything short of playing basketball and baseball for me. Together they'd coached my Little League, put enough oil on my glove to elevate the global energy crisis, and played P-I-G with me (for money). I was a pretty good natural athlete ("You have great hand-eye coordination," they'd always insist), but I didn't like team sports, teammates, or people in general. I took tennis lessons for a few years, but Indian Lake wasn't exactly a hotbed for sports requiring rackets, clubs, or croquet mallets. (If the sport of Cornhole was ever professionalized, however, this would be its home base.)

Too many memories in my room, really, and I was feeling an urge I hadn't felt in a while. Nothing www.nasty.edu with Alba MacBook tonight, although her power light was winking lasciviously at me from the desk. Naw, I wanted to sleep on the floor of Abby's room, like when we were kids and Mom would make popcorn and let us stay up late to watch *Unsolved Mysteries.* Which eventually led to our long-standing fear of being stabbed in our sleep by a ghost.

I grabbed my cell from my nightstand and texted her: "It's your brother, Jay. For the last time, please add my number to your list of contacts. I'm coming over." Send.

Buzz, buzz. Her speedy response: "Whatev . . ."

A few minutes later, I walked into Abby's room armed with my bedding materials. "Mind if I make a floor bed, Sissy Spacek?"

She was trapped underneath a twelve-blanket avalanche: Mt. Sissy. I couldn't see her face, but her long dark hair was splayed across her pillow, the head of her beloved Lazzie Bear visibly gasping for air.

"No," she said, a bit groggily. "Help yourself."

"I think Lazzie is suffocating."

"He's fine."

"Right, he's used to hibernating," I said. "Pa-dum-pum. . . . Thanks, I'll be here all night. On the floor."

I focused on constructing my hallowed floor bed—a complicated art form if there ever was one. The secret to a good night's sleep was the blanket beneath you. Pick a scratchy one, or one too thin, and you were rolling around in agony till the crack. I chose a yellow fleece number from the Martha Stewart collection and folded it in half for extra cushioning. Then came the sheet, the auxiliary blanket, the comforter, and the creepy Martha Stewart–inspired smile of accomplishment. I flopped down, sure this was where I belonged.

"Are you sleeping?" I asked.

"Yes."

"Let's talk."

"No."

How could I lure her into a chat?

"Aren't you dying to address the elephant in the room?" I asked, trying the indirect approach.

"What elephant?" she grumbled. "Only bears."

"I'm serious. What's going on in this house?"

Abby's eyes appeared through a blanket hole and peered out at me. "You really didn't know they were having problems?"

"I had my suspicions, but I thought they were sorting them out. They seemed happy enough. . . ."

"Dad has always been happy," she said sharply.

"Implying what?"

"What do you think? Mom's the one who isn't satisfied."

"Why?"

"Because she needs goo-gobs of attention and will for all eternity," Abby said. "Dad works long hours, and Zeus forbid she's not the Athena of his universe anymore."

Abby was definitely awake now; she was busting out the senior mythology class references and speaking with a hushed fervor that more than revealed whose side she'd taken. And it wasn't our occasionally needy mother's.

"And she's cheating on Dad."

I closed my eyes. The Love Fax had alluded to Mom's discontentment. She'd gone searching. Searching for someone else outside her home, away from us.

"That's why they're separating," Abby added.

"Nooo," I groaned.

"Yes, Jay."

"If so, then who's the lucky guy?"

"Some dude named Keith, I think."

"Some dude named Keith? Well, that seals it. Mom is a boner fide lady of the evening."

"Believe me if you want to," she said.

"How do you know for sure?"

I felt like I was seven years old again: *"Shut up, Jay." "Make me, Abby." "I don't make trash, I burn it."* I was asking my sister to prove our mother was the trash.

"I heard her on the phone a few weeks ago," Abby said. "She didn't know I was home. My car battery died at school. It was raining that day, and I left my freaking headlights on again, so Eric dropped me off before football practice. She was on her cell when she walked in, and I was half asleep on my bed with the door open. Shocker, I know, but I'd forgotten to close it.

Anyway, she was saying—more like whining, 'Not tonight, Keeeeeith. I got home late last night, and there's nothing in the house for dinner but dog food.' And she was laughing like an idiot, like she does when she's drunk, wants attention, or worse—both. You've seen her. You've heard that laugh. It's ridiculous."

I loved that laugh, the same one as Abby's and mine but more womanly (with a hint of cigarette). I'd never heard it as anything other than what it was: an expression of what she thought was funny. But Abby knew when one of her own kind was being flirtatious. She possessed a keen hoochie-mama radar, and Mom had made herself an easy target.

"Maybe he's just a friend," I suggested.

And you say he's just a friend. Oh, baby, yooou . . .

"A friend with a far-too-generous benefits package," Abby said.

"Great, now I have Sour Patch vomit in my mouth," I said.

"Better than Some Dude Named Keith's spooge."

Yes, she went there, and I secretly admired her for it.

"Why didn't you tell me sooner?" I pressed on.

"You and Mom are so close," she said. "Did you really want me to before I was one hundred percent sure?"

"Yes."

No. I really, really didn't want to know about Some Dude Named Keith. But now I knew, and there was no turning back.

TRACK 6

Smells Like Teen Dispirited

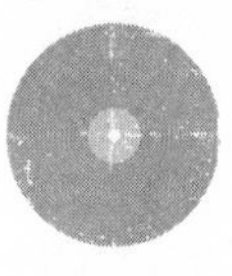

Before I could wake up from my "Very Special Episode of *Hannah Montana*" nightmare, it was Monday morning and I was back at school, my life still very much an ongoing reality show I was trying to quit: "I'm from a Broken Home . . . Get Me Outta Here!" Now I was mixing my TV metaphors? Bad sign.

After Friday, the rest of the weekend had flown. For two people married nineteen years, my parents made no secret of their haste to escape each other. While Abby hid out at her boyfriend Eric's house, Dad, Mom, and I worked all day Saturday at ours, packing Mom's things into her SUV. By Sunday she was settled into her new home on the trailer park range, where the cheesy-poof-stained children played, their heads adorned with construction paper antlers.

So *much* had happened. I hadn't made time to process it, nor had I practiced for the debate, which of course was today.

Staring into my locker at nothing in particular, from the

corner of my eye I spotted Cameo walking toward me. She was wearing a green tank top and those Flo Rida, low-rida apple-bottom jeans that revealed more than just a sliver of her midriff. I tried not to stare at that bull's-eye of flesh, but alas, my female-responsive male genitalia had other ideas. Even with everything so bleeped up, I still wanted to bleep that bleep.

"What's up?" she asked. "How are ya? I didn't hear from you all weekend. Did you get my texts? Too biznastylicious to text me back?"

"Sorry, Cam," I said. "Some stuff was happening at home. . . ."

"Oh, no. Are you okay, Jay?"

She looked concerned, like she felt sorry for me. Awesome. In all the great love stories I'd read, the guy never got the girl by touching her P-spot (i.e., her pity).

"Is it your parents?" she asked, tilting her head toward mine.

Cameo already knew about the Love Fax and the family meeting, so there was no point in lying to her. I managed to mumble the word "separated," and before I could stop her—not that I wanted to—her arms were around me, hands rubbing up and down my shoulder blades. She smelled good. Like hormones. No, what was the word? Pheromones. Whatever, her public display of affection felt nice.

She moved her hands up to my face, placing her cool palms on my cheeks.

"Listen, Jay," she said. "For once, you should let yourself take the easy route. Bail like there's no tomorrow. The debate is less than five minutes away, and *you're not ready.*"

"I haven't even looked at the questions," I admitted.

"Excellent."

"Thanks."

"Not to make you feel worse," Cameo said, as if she wasn't about to, "but I already heard Ms. Lambert cackling down the hall, so she's *definitely ready.* Something about separating the 'choke' from the 'artists' and the 'arti' from the 'choke.'"

"What should I do, then?"

"There's a soul in that Wiccan somewhere," Cameo said. "I could trick her into canceling the debate. I could . . . I could tell her I just got my first period, ever, and I accidentally left the evidence all over the auditorium."

"Are you there, janitor? It's me, Cameo," I said.

"Yes!" she said, nodding. "You wouldn't happen to have a ketchup bottle in your pocket?"

"No, I'm just happy to see you."

Cameo groaned, and I shrugged like it wasn't my fault.

"Using your first period during first period is genius, Cam," I said, taking the opportunity to stare at her chest. "And believable. But Ms. Lambert wouldn't reschedule the debate for anything, not even your blossoming mosquito bites."

The bell rang. The dinner bell of my doom. I was the main course, and everyone knew Mike Hibbard and his baby hadn't missed a meal in years.

TRACK 7

YOU'RE SO GAY (YOU PROBABLY THINK THIS DEBATE IS ABOUT YOU)

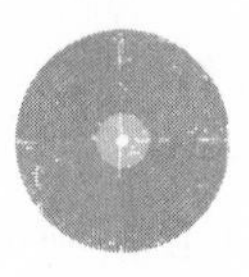

Cameo and I hurried to the auditorium, located in the new addition to our dilapidated school, away from the lockers and classrooms. Apparently, Ms. Lambert wanted the proceedings to look official—officially intimidating. On stage she'd set up two miked podiums, as well as a chair and table with a microphone for herself—arranged so she could ask her questions face-to-candidate but still keep an eye on the untrustworthy freshman attendees.

Most of our class was seated already. Cameo made her way down the aisle toward Jennifer and Sangria; I ambled slowly toward the podium labeled "Baker," hoping an Acme anvil would drop down from the rafters and flatten me in transit.

I stepped up to the stage and made the mistake of peering out into the crowd. My heart started to pound. There were Mike Hibbard's cronies: Brad, Ryan, Andy. A group of ten or so quiet girls dubbed "the gypsies" by class mean girl Rene

Rotrovich (or Rottencrotch, as I preferred) for undisclosed reasons. There were Rene and her minions, a nasty little contingent I was friendly with because of Cameo, touching various body parts of the boy athletes in front of them. Sangria, Jennifer, Greg, Cameo: check. Jennifer gave me a thumbs-up sign, followed quickly by the universal signal that she'd smoked a fatty before school. In testament to that, Greg was fixating on the American flag in the corner. Sangria was sending an illegal text in plain sight. (Jennifer's phone went off a second later; she flipped it open and started laughing.) Last but not least, new girl Caroline sat beside Sangria. Did she just smile at me, or was I hallucinating? She never smiled. A crime against good dentistry, 'cause her teeth were perfect.

"Jay!"

"Yeah?" I said, startled.

I turned around to see Ms. Lambert emerge from the sea of stage curtains. She was dressed in her usual bewitching garb, direct from the Stevie Nicks collection. Layer upon black layer of silky fabric draped her short-'n'-stout body. Her curly, frizzy, defiantly gray hair framed her cheeks like a lion's mane—an interesting contrast to the porcine features of her face. She was a Babe of the pig variety. In her forties, she wore no makeup to hide it. As she put it, "I prefer to let the natural earth tones of my skin shine through. Ha!" Rather than waste time being insecure, she embraced her butt-fugliness with admirable moxie.

"Are you ready or what, President-Wannabe Baker?" she said, smirking and putting her hands on her hips. "I ain't got all day for y'all to sputter your teenage nonsense. We absolutely must adjourn before third-period theater class starts; otherwise, Mr. Collins and his drama goslings will pitch a hissy. Ha!"

"I don't really feel like debating today."

"Tough noogies."

"Can you put that in layman's terms?" I quipped, but it sounded more sad than sarcastic.

"Is everything okay, Jay?" Ms. Lambert asked, flipping into teacher mode.

Although outwardly evil, she *did* have a soft spot beneath those robes somewhere, especially for me.

"Of course," I said, flashing my best fake smile.

"Do you have Mike's body bag ready?" she ventured.

"Thank goodness Hefty comes in husky."

"There's my favorite smart-ass!" she said. "But watch that you don't cross that line on stage, Jay. I've only known you a few weeks, but that doesn't mean I'm not privy to how you and Mr. Hibbard feel about each other. Keep it on the up-and-up and do your best. If that's not enough, at least it will be easy for me to count the votes."

Ms. Lambert headed over to her table and sat down pointedly so everyone knew to be quiet. Putting on her tortoiseshell glasses (made from genuine tortoise), she said into the microphone, "Welcome, my favorite frosh, to the First Annual Freshman Class Presidential Debate. First off, if you throw so much as a pencil shaving at me, I will suspend your *Jersey Shore*–watching selves and call your parents daily to ensure your *situation* includes watching C-SPAN with soundproof headphones on."

She looked pleased with herself.

"To clarify—for those of you already struggling to follow along, ahem, Jennifer—there will be absolutely no talking during the debate. Say hello to Ms. Riddell over there in the corner of the auditorium. She'll be keeping an all-seeing eye on you, too."

A collective "Hi, Ms. Riddell!" rang out.

"Will you marry me, Ms. Riddell?" a boy cried out.

"No talking!" Ms. Riddell screamed bitterly.

The room fell silent again.

Standing six-foot-one and weighing in at half the cost of a McDonald's extra-value meal (two-fifty and counting), Sandy Riddell was mad as hell about her gym-teaching lot in life—and she wasn't going to take any of our crap.

"I thought I told y'all no talking," Ms. Lambert said. "Ha! Thank you for your services, Ms. Riddell. They are *mucho* appreciated. I'm sure Andy Moore will write you a heartfelt apology letter in detention today."

Andy "No Relation to Mandy" Moore, member of Mike's posse and the identified marriage proposer, looked miffed.

Ms. Lambert continued. "As you know, frosh, you already narrowed down the candidate pool to two during last Monday's primary election. For those of you unfamiliar with their lovely faces, we have Jay Baker on the left and Mike Hibbard on the right."

Mike, sweating like a pig in a Snuggie, glared at me with something akin to murderous hatred in his eyes. Normally, I could match his intensity Itchy for Scratchy, but not today. I started to panic. My phone buzzed, and I knew it had to be her.

I snuck a look at the screen: "I can still get my period. Aunt Flow lives just around the river bend."

Bloody hell, I wanted so badly to type, "Yes, Cam! Deliver those periodicals!" But then menopause struck. . . .

"The debate starts now, my little lamb chops," Ms. Lambert said, and I quickly snapped my phone shut. "The first question goes to . . . drumroll . . . Mike."

She turned to him. "Mike. What's the first change you'd implement as freshman class president?"

Mike: "Um, I'm not impressed with the cafeteria's food, and neither are my boys," he said. "We need the cooks to go to cooking class and learn how to fry us up something good. I mean, how many things can be made from the same chicken patty?"

He stopped. That was his answer. Mike's fan box cheered until Ms. Riddell's looming shadow stole their sunshine.

"Interesting response, Mike," Ms. Lambert said. "Let's hope things go a little better for you on the next question."

"Jay, do you have a rebuttal?" she asked, turning to me.

"The chicken patty is an institution in this school," I began. "It's fun to see what dishes it will show up in. Ha-ha."

No one laughed. Someone near the back said, "No, it's not."

"Sure it is," I continued. "Just the other day, I was surprised to discover it beneath the noodles and sauce of my chicken Parmesan. Anyway, isn't it lame to focus on food, when there are far more important issues like . . . like . . ."

Universal health care? I sounded weird, awkward, constipated. I stared out at my class. They definitely didn't approve of this message. Understandably. What was I saying?

"Like . . . pop machines. I could really go for a Mountain Dew right now. . . ."

"Thanks, Jay," Ms. Lambert said skeptically. "Is that all?"

"Yeah."

Punt! Go NASCAR! Did the racing community popularity of my favorite soda save my answer? Did I nab the Future Farmers of America vote? Fizzle. Doubtful. I looked toward my friends for support. Jennifer gave me a thumbs-up sign again, taking a swig from the twenty-ounce she kept permanently stored in her Powerpuff Girls purse.

And where was I again? Oh, yeah: here. Snap out of it, Jay.

"Let's move on," Ms. Lambert said. "Jay, what do you think of the school's plans to move the band room into a virtual cubbyhole to make way for a more spacious weight room?"

Here was my chance. Rather than wait for Mike to strike, I could preempt him with a gutterball of my own—serve notice I wasn't going to let his muffin top me without a fight.

"Clearly, the increased opportunity for cardio will benefit some," I said, making sure everyone saw me look in Mike's direction.

A few snickers rang out.

"Jay, don't make me get my yardstick," Ms. Lambert said. "Answer the question appropriately, or you'll be disqualified."

"Sorry. Band, football, doesn't matter. Moving isn't easy on anyone . . ."

With my body stuck in the moment, my thoughts crept off the stage and back to yesterday . . .

Moving Mom. Packing up her assorted fire hazards: favorite blanket, heating pad, microwavable neck warmer, and the ancient toaster that I insisted she take even though she'd configured it to brown my Pop Tarts to perfection. Oh, and don't forget the bull skull she'd purchased during her short-lived Southwestern phase. ("Something died so you could have this," I said, packing it up.) Check.

"Sometimes the school has to make tough decisions . . ."

"Do you want to come over tonight, Buckwheat?" Mom asked when we were finished. "I have digital cable. We could order a movie. Have you seen Paranormal Activity*?"*

Part of me wanted to say, "You mean what you've been doing with Some Dude Named Keith?" out of loyalty to Dad.

"I'll grab the popcorn," I said instead, afraid of what would happen to Mom's handle-with-care psyche if I declined.

"JAY?" Ms. Lambert said.

"Yeah, sorry . . . lost my train of thought."

I wasn't sure how long I'd trailed off, but the J-Train had careened off the tracks. My face was hot. My head—kind of big for my body, anyway—felt like a bowling ball on my neck.

"Uh, I'm gonna pass," I said.

Out. I'm gonna pass out.

"You were saying something about tough decisions, right?" she prompted. "What did you mean by that?"

"Tough decisions are . . . difficult. I have no idea. Next question. White flag."

I held up my paper of questions and waved it.

Love Fax: "Bear with me for a little longer." M*A*S*H. *Hot tub. Kissy-kissy. Trial separation. Buckwheat. Holiday Shores. Some Dude Named Keith. Some dude named Keith. Some Douchebag Named Keith who'd ruined everything.*

I backed away from the podium and sat down on the hard

folding chair behind it. Somebody, quick, get that large showbiz hook and pull me off stage. My Shirley temples were throbbing, and . . . please, no. My eyes were beginning to well up. The salty water crept dangerously around my lower lids. Lashes, don't fail me now. Thinking maybe I could pass for tired, I put my head down and smeared everything around the best I could. I must have looked ridiculous.

Mike could smell blood, and he didn't wait for Ms. Lambert to offer the chance for rebuttal.

"Evidently," he began, "this topic is a very difficult one for my opponent. He's probably wanted to join the band for years, but found it difficult to—let's just say—come out of the closet?"

"Mike!" Ms. Lambert screamed.

Laughter filled the auditorium, echoing off the walls and bouncing back into my ears.

"He still can," Mike continued, but he was losing his nerve. "No one is stopping him. Just like no one can stop the football team from winning State this year. What up, Lakers?!"

"Mike Hibbard!" Ms. Lambert raged. "There's quite enough thinly veiled homophobia in rural Ohio as it is—your thick-skulled campaign contributions are equal parts offensive and unnecessary. In fact, your next debate will be with Principal Boyer over why he shouldn't suspend you like Beckham. This assembly of ignorami, is over. Everyone report to your first-period classes, *immediately*!"

The tears in my eyes had quickly evaporated, anger left in their place. Did he actually think he was going to get away with that? It was more important to ruin me than win the election? Wait a minute . . . Mike might be onto something. As everyone began to scatter, I stood and grabbed the microphone, the accompanying screeching sound causing them to turn back toward the stage.

"Perhaps my opponent needs to stop burying his inappropriate feelings for his mom underneath a mound of food and drop a few on his own, without the help of a weight room. At this rate, he's gonna need a wheelchair by . . . tomorrow. But, hey, if an STD with an Oedipus complex is what you're looking for from a president, please cast your vote for Mike and contract a case of the Herp today. I quit."

I walked off the back of the stage and out the rear exit. I'd lost my family, I'd lost the election, and now I'd definitely lost Cameo.

"You will," she said. "Maybe not now, but when the officer my choosing puts his or her stamp on all your class events, ı'll no doubt feel otherwise."

"Puts his/her stamp on what?" I said. "Building the Home-ning Game float? Go for it. In fact, allow me to nominate ne Rotrovich. She has future political scandal written all over ."

"You can do better, Jay," she said, disappointed. "You could e done this. People would like you if you'd just let them. You ı't need all the bells and whistles to distract them."

"Look," I said, "I only ran to impress someone, and that got —you guessed it—nowhere. I don't care about the stupid hman class, this stupid school. I said it at the podium: I quit. east you don't have to count the votes."

Irreversibly irritated now, she said, "I'll inform Mr. Collins you're a prime candidate for the drama squad. And de-tion, too, for that matter."

"Yeah, please do," I said. "I'm really looking forward to hing both."

walked out the door.

TRACK 8

I Could Drink a Case of Dew

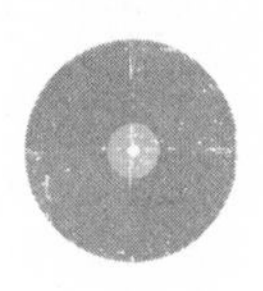

Almost immediately afterward, Cameo texted me: "Oh, brother-from-another-mother, where art thou? You okay?"

I texted back: "Hark, the sound of toilets flushing. In the bathroom by the library. The handicapped stall. I'm retarded."

Her response: "I prefer the handicapped stall, too. Spacious and less peeage on the seatage."

Cameo and I used to write dirty poems back and forth to one another in sixth grade. Her classic, "If you sprinkle before you tinkle, be a sweetie and wipe the seaty," was a cause she still believed in. The apprehension of dump-and-run bandits was another. (From the desk of Jay Baker: "If you squat and make a poopy, flush that feces, don't be stoopy.") E.g., last Tuesday she informed me, "I know for a fact that Stasha Henderson took an epic shadoob in my fave stall and didn't flush."

Buzz, buzz. Another text from her: "I still have the spare set of keys to Wade's pickup. Meet me in the parking lot in three minutes."

"Is it the green one with the 'She thinks my tractor's sexy' bumper sticker? I'll be there in two." Send.

I had to get it together. Hiding in the bathroom like this, jeez: I was such a little girl. Poor, poor Baby Baker had been humiliated in front of the entire student body. What would I do now? Eat my lunches in a random-ass phone booth like DJ Tanner on *Full House?* Become addicted to caffeine pills à la Jessie Spano on *Saved by the Bell?* Pull a Joey and drown my sorrows in *Dawson's Creek?*

I ran water over my face and wiped it with the harsh sandpaper from the dispenser. My hair looked like unfreshly mowed grass, my eyes like Jennifer's after seizing her last chance to toke Mary Jane's dying ember. Otherwise, I was on cloud nine and living it up with the Charmin bears.

I walked out of the bathroom and darted quickly down the hall toward the nearest exit. It was by the gym, which ran parallel to the library and away from the classrooms, so I didn't think any teachers would be around. Anyway, I had study hall second period with the school's football coach, Mr. Ellington, who stared at game tape all day and could barely be bothered to take attendance. I was just about to push in the bar of the faux Emergency Exit door (it never went off) when a different alarm sounded from behind me.

"Jay Baker!"

Suck on a sheep's teat and call me the Lord's shepherd. It was Ms. Lambert.

She walked—no, hovered—toward me, eyes blazing and

robes flowing behind her. Was someone blow
from up above?

"What in the name of Howard Dean was
there?" she demanded.

"I dunno," I said dumbly.

"I think you do."

"I'm going through some personal problems

"Like what?" she asked. "And this better be

"I'd say it's more suitable for *Tyra*."

"Just talk."

I hesitated, not really wanting to get into
the wherewithal to get out of it.

"My parents are probably getting a D-
didn't have time to prepare for today. I *di*
ticipate in that stupid debate in the first pl
freshmen, not politicians. And Mike Hibba
shi . . . swine. Whatever."

Ms. Lambert chewed on my pathos for
thoughtful.

"I'm sorry to hear about your parents,
really am. Admittedly, the debate was an
wrong. Mike will get what he deserves. As
personal note, stooping to that childish leve
intelligence, and it's certainly not going to e
one, let alone win an election."

"Objection, boring," I said under my bre

"Heard that. Overruled."

"Honestly, I could give a flying about
dent," I said.

TRACK 9

I Kissed a Girl and She Wasn't That Crazy About It

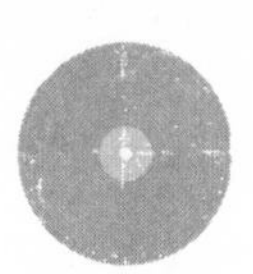

Ms. Lambert didn't follow me out. She must have felt sorry enough for me to figure we could deal with the repercussions of my public meltdown later. Plus, she probably reasoned that a freshman without a car wouldn't be going too far. She wasn't aware of Cameo and the unconvincing fake ID she'd obtained from Chippewa, the seedy north-side-area community of Indian Lake where such contraband could be purchased (from Jennifer's house—her parents made them). Cameo's alias: a skanky-looking physical unlikeness named Eliza Doolittle.

I spotted Wade's truck already running in the parking lot. I reached it, opened the door, and slid in beside Cam.

"Eliza Doolittle, at your service," she said, saluting me.

"You're looking strikingly X-rated today, Eliza."

"Thanks, love!"

"Welcome."

"Hair toss!" she said, tossing the blond hair she'd let loose.

I was relieved to see her acting like nothing had changed.

"What took you so long?" she asked. "I've gone through half a Toby Keith CD already."

"Baaaah. I had a run-in with Lambert before escaping."

"Great, now all three of us are implicated," she said. "Cameo isn't going to like this. . . ."

"I'll cover for you and Cameo, Eliza," I promised.

"How?"

"Haven't gotten that far."

"Let's worry about you for now, Jay," she said. "Cam and Eliza have been around the school-skipping block a few times, if you catch my drift."

"I think I caught it," I said. "Even though the Stetson scent in here is pretty strong."

"Ugh, tell me about it. Roll down your window. Let's drive for a little."

A driving pro after years of terrorizing others on the bumper cars of Kings Island, Cameo effortlessly weaved Wade's truck around the hilly roads of the Logan County countryside while singing some fairy princess Taylor Swift song I hadn't heard before. I stared out the window, watched the barns, cornfields, and simple houses passing me by.

"We moved Mom out yesterday," I said.

Cameo stopped singing. "What? Where is she living?"

"Holiday Shores."

Once again, Cameo's blue eyes were full of compassion (instead of the passion I would have preferred). "I'm so sorry, Jay."

"About the transportable accommodations, or my parents?"

"You know what I mean," she said. "I can't believe you even showed up for school today."

"Yeah, and I'm not ready to go back."

"Me either."

"Wanna see her pad?" I asked impulsively.

"Sure, why not?"

"Turn left on Thirty-three. She's at work, and you aren't the only one with a spare set of keys."

Ten minutes later, Cameo pulled Wade's pickup underneath Mom's carport. We walked around the side of the trailer and through the "Florida room" that Mom had furnished with two plastic chairs. I slipped the key into the door, and we entered.

"Home, sweet double-wide."

"This place is legit, Jay," Cameo said, looking around. "I'm liking your mom's eclectic decorating taste. Nate Berkus has nothing on her."

"What's a Nate Berkus?"

"Never mind. And look, she bought you the plasma you've always wanted," Cam said, pointing to the fifty-inch TV that looked oddly gigantic in the small living room.

I took to the couch and turned on my silver lining. Cameo helped herself to the refrigerator, grabbing two Mountain Dews, and returned to sit beside me on the overstuffed love seat.

"Sooooo," she said, "let's talk. Let's work the love, the pain, the whole darn thang out in that messy li'l head of yours."

"Let's not and say we watched TV."

"I insist. We can explore the debate, your parents, everything. It'll help you grow and shiz. Join me on the path to self-realization. I'll be the Connie Chung to your Maury Povich."

"I'm busy, Connie. I'll be sure to chung you with my wang later, though."

I turned up the volume passive-aggressively.

"I suppose I can take a hint," she lied, using her soft voice—the one I could never deny.

I looked over at her profile. Her cute little snub nose. Her nice lips—thinner on the sides, but just the right amount of curvature in the middle. I desperately wanted to kiss them. Forget what was happening at home.

"What are you looking at?"

"Nothing," I said. "Your face looks weird."

"So does yours," she said. "Quit sucking your cheeks in. You look like an anorexic version of that guy on *Gossip Girl.* The one with the man-bangs."

"Speaking of man-bangs, I wonder if Gossip Girl will alert the media that my mom is cheating on my dad with Some Dude Named Keith."

She turned to me, shocked. "What?"

"Yep," I said matter-of-factly.

"You're just full of surprises today," she said. "How do you know for sure?"

"My sister heard her talking to him on the phone. Everything makes sense now. The Love Fax from Dad. The late nights spent at Whereabouts Nowhere. It's all there: one big long

Lifetime unoriginal movie being filmed as we speak. And, yes, before you say anything, I'm the after-school special."

"Crap, Jay," she said, reaching out for my hand. "I don't know what to say."

How about you just leave my hand alone so I don't start breathing heavily and humping your leg? But her fingers touched mine then, closing around them.

Sparks shot out of my head; my brain crackled. Something inside me said, "Screw it." Or did it say *her*? I reached for Cameo, wanting her closer to me, craving that human connection. I needed her to tell me I wasn't alone in this, that it wasn't that big of a deal, the end of the world, that my mom and dad didn't want to watch sitcoms together anymore and pretend life was a hunky-Dory-Finding-Nemo Disney movie.

I brought Cameo's arms and torso in tightly to me, and she knew enough to let me hold her. What was really twenty seconds seemed like an eternity, and forever was how long I needed it to be. *Couldn't we just stay like this?* Reluctantly, I broke the hug, but only so I could move my face in closer proximity to hers. I could see the familiar dusting of freckles on her nose, the flecks of gold in her blue eyes, the faint cracks of her lips. I moved mine closer to hers, then pressed forward, unthinking. I found her mouth and gently wedged my lips between hers, began to search for something. Consent. Reciprocation. Some sign of life on her end that this felt as right to her as it did to me, that this wasn't like kissing her brother. My eyes were closed, mostly because I didn't want to see her reaction. Her mouth almost left mine for a second, the kiss, the girl, fading.

But then she seemed to change her mind. We switched positions and she enveloped my top lip with both of hers, again and again, to the point where she was almost biting me. My tongue flicked across hers when something seemed to startle her. She jolted back as if hit by lightning, looking absolutely stunned.

"Oh, my God!" she cried, pressing her fingers to her lips.

"Was it that bad?"

"Huh?" she said, not really listening. "No, we should go. C'mon. I have to go. . . ."

She grabbed her purse from the coffee table and hurried out the door, no doubt preparing to back-handspring away from any future interaction with me.

Great. Awesome. I'd freaked out my best friend trying to get my freak on. What else could I ruin today?

TRACK 10

Let It Bleep

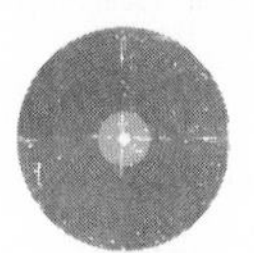

The house was empty when I arrived home after school; Mom in Holiday Shores exile, Dad still working, and Abby at volleyball practice. In the kitchen feasting on Siamese Pop Tarts, I couldn't help but remember the twin tears running down my sister's cheeks.

I grabbed a Mountain Dew and a Ziploc full of Skittles (Mom Ziplocked all solid foods), then walked into the living room to try my hand and arm at a new Wii game she'd bought me recently: the ironically titled Cooking Mama.

The game made no flipping sense. Didn't come with directions, either, except for this empty, oft-repeated promise from Cooking Mama herself: "Don't worry! Mama will fix it!" Mama wasn't helpful. I kept flubbing up my soufflé, chopping and dicing frantically with my Wiimote to no avail, my frustration building until I threw the stupid Wiidget against the wall. The batteries popped out limply.

I sat down on the couch. For the second time today, I bent my head down to my knees in anguish. But this time I let the tears I'd held in for three days fall into my hands.

Embarrassing. Once I recovered my composure, I took a good look at my surroundings. Mom hadn't been gone a week, and the family room—the entire house, actually—was a "certified OSHA violation," as my bio teacher, Mr. Fulton, would say when someone (Cameo) didn't clean up his/her lab space according to Occupational Safety and Health Administration code. Half-empty—definitely not half-full, in my current mood—pop cans littered all surfaces. Fruit Roll-Up wrappers traversed the floor like tumbleweeds. Buffy had scattered her bone remnants across the carpet, to be expected and tolerated.

I started cleaning everything in sight. I swept, I mopped, I conquered. I was Mr. Clean on Adderall, even scrubbing my latest irritable bowel syndrome attack off the innocent downstairs toilet I'd defaced. (Yeah, I actually do have IBS. Hence my preoccupation with poop. One couldn't go through life as A-obsessed, type A, and anal retentive as I had without their intestines feeling the effects. Since the second grade, I'd been one scoop of ice cream away from a Hershey squirt.)

It felt good to be busy and productive, to forget about the debate and my parents for the time being. But what to do about dinner?

Well, I'd seen Mom cook spaghetti a million times. *Eat your heart out, Cooking Mama; I don't need any help from you.* I grabbed some hamburger meat from the freezer, thawed it in the microwave, placed it in the saucepan for browning, started boiling the water, cracked the noodles in half, preheated the oven for the all-important Texas toast side dish.

Before I knew it, I heard a key jingling in the lock—then Dad calling my name. At seven thirty? Pretty early for him.

"What in the world?" he said, entering the kitchen. "Is that my son . . . cooking?"

"Is that my dad . . . not working?"

"Big Dad, kiddies' pal," he said, loosening his power tie.

"My culinary skills are about to knock your tasseled loafers off, Dad."

"It smells great, buddy," he said, surveying the premises and noting how much cleaner it looked. He took a seat on one of the bar stools, looking like he wanted to talk. "How'd the debate go today?"

I didn't have the energy to mince meat *and* words.

"I bombed in front of everyone, called out Mike Hibbard for being the potbellied poser he is, stormed off the stage in a fit of awkward rage, and then skipped school for an hour. It was quite an impressive display of destructive behavior. Oh, and Ms. Lambert gave me detention for the rest of the week."

Eyebrows raised, Dad was looking mighty surprised by my sudden rebellious streak. Normally such a square peg, I'd gone and dug myself a round grave.

"Let's eat," he said slowly. "I need to think about this."

The spaghetti was edible, but neither Dad nor I had much of an appetite. Once we finished loading the dishwasher, he suggested we move our discussion out into the garage so that he could have a "smoky-smoke." He walked toward the door, whistling for the dog (and me), and Buffy miraculously awoke from her comatose state and followed slowly behind—one of her Sam's Club biscuit boxes was located near his cigarette cartons.

"So what's really going on?" he asked, opening the garage doors to air out the room before lighting up.

"What do you think, Dad?" I said. "What in tarnation could be bothering me right now?"

He took a puff and threw a couple of treats Buffy's way. They scattered on the slick cement floor, and she lazily dragged her body forward to reach them with her mouth.

"I've been meaning to check in with you sooner, buddy," he said apologetically. "I'm not thrilled that what's going on between your mom and me might be causing you to act out. Your home life is changing, so rather than sit back and let it change you, you're beating it to the punch. That's why you're in self-destruct mode, right?"

Something like that.

"But trust me," he went on, "it's not worth throwing away your extracurricular activities—the stuff you enjoy doing—because you're upset with Big Dad."

"Student government was never gonna be my cup of Dew, Dad. Didn't inherit your gift for public speaking, I guess. Exhibit IBS is still being featured against the toilet. It's abstract, and I couldn't scrub it all off."

"Then did running for class president have anything to do with . . . someone else?" Dad hedged.

"Like whom?"

"Cameo?"

"Heil Hitler, I'm going to draw tiny mustaches on Abby's college applications."

Dad gave me *the look*. "Your sister didn't tell me anything. You left Alba MacBook in the living room the other night and I snooped."

Proof that turnabout really was fair play.

"We need to talk about Cameo . . ."

"Why Cameo?" I asked, flustered. "What about Mom?"

I paused, unsure if I should let the IBS hit the fan, too.

"Did she really cheat on you, Dad?"

Banzai! Sick of tiptoeing around the elephant in the room, I'd gone kamikaze on its Dumbo-ass and asked Dad to confirm Mom's betrayal. A more sensible person would have sought out the source, but I'd always protected Mom.

Surprisingly, Dad didn't take his time responding.

"Yes" was all he said, but the pain inside the word told a much longer story. Even a confident, accomplished career man like Jim Baker could be shattered by his wife checking out a copy of another guy's Moby Dick.

"With Some Dude Named Keith?" I asked.

"Yes, Keith Parnell."

Keith Parnell. Keith *Parnell*. Some Dude Named Keith was Cameo Appearance Parnell's dad!

TRACK 11

The Loser Takes It All

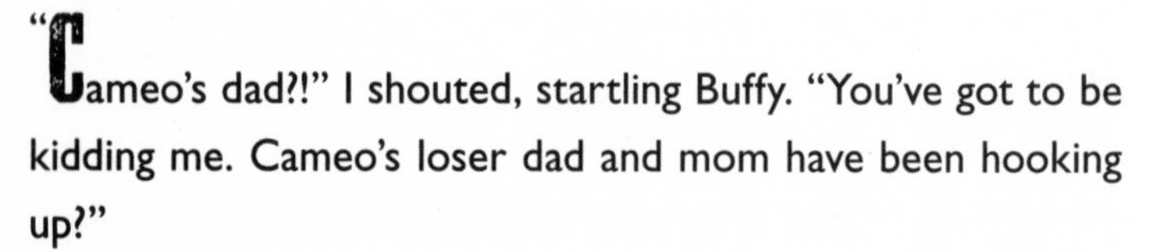

"Cameo's dad?!" I shouted, startling Buffy. "You've got to be kidding me. Cameo's loser dad and mom have been hooking up?"

Keith Parnell ran a DUI-prevention taxi service, which meant he circled the lakeside bars in a van labeled ".08? Need A Lift?" looking for drunk people to ferry home. Perhaps he could have passed this off as a noble profession if he hadn't been using it as a red herring to avoid DUIs himself.

"When were you or Mom going to tell me? When did *you* find out?"

"About a month ago."

"A month ago?"

"I found out your mom was cheating on me a month ago," he clarified. "She didn't tell me it was with Keith until last week. And I wasn't sure how to tell you, if I should, or if that was your mom's place—so it's been on the back burner for the last few days, and I'm really sorry about that. Based on what happened at school today, I think the sooner we get it all out there, the better."

A month ago. She'd told him right after the Love Fax, probably. Had that been the catalyst, the cig that fell on the camel's crack and broke Mom's back to the point where she couldn't bear the weight of her own guilt anymore?

"Why him?" I asked, on the verge of losing it. "Why Keith Parnell?"

"I have no idea," Dad said, shrugging his shoulders miserably. "They met at one of Abby's volleyball games a year ago. I had a late appointment, so your mom was working at the concession stand by herself. It was busy, so I guess Keith took it upon himself to help her out."

I'm sure he did, I thought, my mind whirring: *"Can I take your order, Keith?" "Yeah, I'd like a Kim Sandwich." "Extra juicy?" "Yes, please." "Pickle?" "Thanks, but I'll be providing that."*

Thankfully, Dad spoke again.

"To borrow from the most overused phrase in sports these days, it is what it is, Jay. It happened. To me, the *who* part never mattered."

"*He's* a home-wrecking bastard," I said. "That's who he is. Just because Keith assisted Mom in making a few shredded-chicken sandwiches, doesn't give the motherfu—"

"Buddy."

". . . Motherfinagler the right to ruin our lives."

Dad was quiet for a minute. Talking about the easiness of Mom's virtue was definitely hard for him, but I could tell he was wrestling with something else.

"You know," he said, "your mom has a hand in this, too."

"Uh-huh, it has a wedding ring on it."

For good measure, Mom also wore the wedding rings of her mom and her mom's mom around her neck—both maternal grandmothers had passed away before Abby and I were born.

"I hesitate to bring this up now," Dad said, "but I suppose there's never going to be a right time."

"Yeah?"

"Well, if your mom and I don't get back together," he said, lighting another cigarette, "I'd prefer it if you and Abby lived with me."

Of course Dad was bringing this up now. He knew how I'd be feeling about Mom in this moment, and he was human—a father scared of losing his kids and everything else he'd known for nineteen-plus years.

I walked over and grabbed a Mountain Dew from the garage refrigerator.

"So then let's be honest, Dad," I said, sitting back down and flipping the tab. "What are the chances of you and Mom getting back together?"

"Unlike your dog, I'd say they're pretty slim," he said. "But we don't want to make any rash decisions, especially when it comes to you kids."

We sat there for a while, him smoking, me sipping, Buffy sleeping.

"I'm not saying your mom is a bad person, Jay. I'm a little confused about who my wife is right now, but I know she'll always be a good mother."

"You don't have to do that, Dad. Stick up for her, I mean. She should stick up for herself."

Just then, a dark car pulled into the driveway. A black Lexus, to be exact, the vehicle of choice for the surreal housewife behind the moniker "Cameo Appearance Parnell."

"Oh, for the love of God," I said. "Cameo's mom?"

"Don't look at me," Dad said. "I didn't invite her."

TRACK 12

You're Just Like a Pill I Just Swallowed

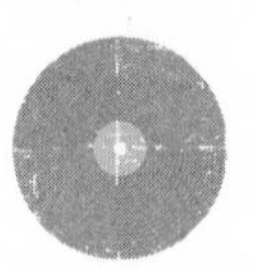

The driver's-side door opened and Cameo stepped out. I was going Jaywire on the inside, but I couldn't resist taking inventory of Cam's exterior. Her tight end was looking resplendent in her red and white Indian Lake booty shorts, designed to have drooling dorkuses like me reaching for comic books to place in front of our crotches. Her skin, fresh from her cheerleading "workout," glistened in the light emanating from the garage.

"If it isn't Cameo Parnell," Dad said jovially. "How are you?"

Being that he was a financial sales expert, Dad could recover quickly from any sticky situation. "Always have a contingency plan, Jay," he'd say whenever I attempted to Chapter 13 my way out of something. He even waved at Cameo's mom, who remained in the car and didn't wave back, instead concentrating on her BlackBerry. So, if Mrs. Parnell hadn't stopped by to shoot the breeze, then why was Cameo here?

"Hi, Mr. Baker," Cameo said. "I'm fine. Hurt myself at practice today, though. A leaping herkie went all kinds of wrong. Should've gone with the pretzel."

She lifted her leg up and touched her hand to her knee.

"That's too bad," Dad said, doing the same.

"Isn't it?" she said, laughing. "Anyway, I'm at the top of the pyramid this year, and in case a tragic cheering accident should ever happen, I'm thinking of taking out a policy with you and naming your son the benefactor."

Her fishy shtick was aggravating *me*, a noted shtick offender. Maybe I was a little bitter that she'd rebuffed me earlier with no explanation. Full disclosure: Now that I knew our parents were bumping uglies, I didn't know what to feel for the girl I'd loved for so long.

"A girl after my own heart," Dad said, walking toward the door. "I'll let you two talk, but you're welcome to come inside for some of Jay's spaghetti, Cameo."

He raised his eyebrows in her direction: *Jay cooked.* She raised hers at me: *You cooked?* I stared back blankly, refusing to play along as Dad shut the door.

"You know, don't you?" she said immediately.

"How to make spaghetti? Or about your dad canoodling with my mom? Don't wanna get my pastas confused."

"The grosser one."

"Why didn't you tell me sooner, Cam?"

"I wasn't sure until today. I mean, I had my suspicions—Some Dude Named *Keith*, all his alleged chiropractor appointments, the fights with my mom about him spending too much money on random things like deluxe heating pads. When

I saw that unnecessary space heater next to your mom's recliner at the trailer, it all came crashing down on me like whoa at an inopportune time. You know, during the wha-wha."

"The what? Never mind, so basically your dad is exploiting my mom's weakness for personal heating devices and using it to his advantage."

The disgusted look on my face was illuminated by the Lexus's annoying headlights. I made an impatient flipping motion toward Cameo's mom to turn them off, but she was still looking at her BlackBerry.

"Don't bother," Cam said. "I pried out all I could from her earlier, but then she took a Mother's Little Helper, turned on Bejeweled Blitz—an app I never should have downloaded for her—and refused to talk. She's pretty out of it. I'm not even sure she knows we're here."

Cameo and I sat down in the white plastic chairs typically occupied by Mom and Dad. I put my hands in my hair and tugged.

"What about your dad? What did he say?"

"Dad wasn't home."

Cameo shifted uncomfortably in the chair, drawing her knees up to her chest.

"Mom said this isn't the first time Dad has Whoopi'd his Goldberg elsewhere, and it certainly wouldn't be the last. I guess she's used to it. As long as my grandpa gives her money for pills, she wouldn't care if a bird shat on her head and then nested there. She's an empty vessel. Ladies and gentlemen, my mother. For better or worse, I can't divorce *her.*"

I could think of a few empty vessels that needed filling

right about then. The *Niña*, the *Pinta*, and the collective cranial space of the Parnells.

"You know, maybe I'm a bit emo right now, but you seem exceptionally calm, Cam. Our parents have been engaging in a raunchy affair for Lord knows how long, and you and I are now stepsiblings in the making. Aren't you embarrassed? Why aren't you having more of a reaction?"

"That's your job," she said defensively.

Finally, she was being real.

"What's that supposed to mean?"

"Ever since we were kids, when you and I have a crisis to control, you react, and I help you deal."

"Funny, I don't remember asking for your help."

"Whatever, take your anger out on me. You know my parents have always been two retainer fees shy of a divorce. What am I supposed to do? Please, tell me, because caring has never done me any good. I feel bad for you. Your parents were—are—the real thing. My dad is probably just a passing fling in your mom's life. He certainly is in mine. He's a walking, talking disappointment machine, so your family has nothing to worry about. He won't last long. There, is that enough of a reaction for you?"

Damn.

"Yeah, that'll do," I said. "Sorry, Cam . . . I just—"

"Forget it."

Cameo readjusted her ponytail, composing herself. "Have you talked to your mom?"

"I don't know how to have that conversation," I said.

"You need to talk to her," she persisted.

Silence.

"Jay?"

"I think I'm done discussing our parents."

"So what do you want to talk about? Us? The kiss?"

My cheeks burned. "I haven't thought much about it, Cam."

Of course I had, but I was trying to protect myself. I didn't know if I trusted Cameo, who was now looking hurt by my bogus irreverence. I was such a bad actor; I couldn't believe she was buying it.

"I just don't want things to be weird," she said.

"This conversation isn't the antidote."

"Considering all that's happened, we should probably have it," she said. "What it meant to me . . . it meant . . ." Cameo stopped, biting her lip again.

"Nothing," I said, rejecting myself for her. "You should go. I'm tired. You're off the hook. The kiss was definitely a mistake."

"Fine," she said, storming off toward the car.

TRACK 13

Since U Been Gone, I Went Ahead and Ripped One

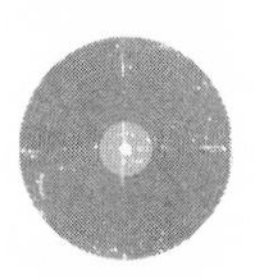

That night was obviously another floor bed occasion.

I entered Abby's room noisily enough to avoid knife-wielding ghost status. The lights were off, but someone was home underneath the covers, the rays from her cell phone shining from beneath the material as her peeps flooded her with pointless texts. She said nothing as I began folding, refolding, and fluffing my floor bed. Not ready to chat yet. It could take her several hundred bottles of beer to warm up, but I was determined to wait her out.

La-da-da-da-di-da-da-da-daaaah.

I soon grew bored and decided to insert myself into her text queue: "Hi, it's me, Jay. I'm on the floor. FYI, I just farted, it's rancid, and it's making its way upward RIGHT NOW. I'm relieved, but mostly just embarrassed. Let's talk about it. And about Cameo."

Ah, fart jokes. A common denominator bringing everyone closer together since Adam let forth the first one in front of Eve. They were irresistible in their smelly nature; whether you laid one or you were the recipient, mutual laughter was inevitable. I'd long since deduced that they were particularly potent when dealing with my sister. Even she couldn't ignore the tickling of her funny bone if I sang something classy like "I just ripped one, I just ripped one for the first time" to the tune of "Since U Been Gone." "I Just Ripped One" was number two on the iTunes chart in my head, and it always would be.

A few minutes later, Abby texted back: "FYI, even Lazzie gets sick of hearing you talk about Cameo. It makes him want to return the farting favor."

My verbal response: "Tell Lazzie that bear farts aren't welcome in these parts."

She laughed, placing her phone on the nightstand.

"Soooo, Mom and Keith Parnell. Aka, my unrequited love's loser father. Have you heard?"

"It's all over school already," she said. "Eric knew for weeks and kept it from me until today. Said he wasn't sure, even though I guess he saw Mom riding with Keith in that stupid-ass DUI-mobile."

There was a world of hurt and embarrassment in Abby's voice because of Mom and Eric. Mom was a given. But what good was a boyfriend who was scared to tell you the truth? Who couldn't even return sixty of her brain cells with nine of his own? No wonder she kept things close to the vest (and refused to be seen in one).

"I suppose we should talk to Mom about it, eventually," I said.

As in tomorrow, because I was supposed to have dinner with her at Holiday Shores. I didn't want to go alone and was working up to asking Abby.

"She's called me four times tonight," Abby said. "She knew we'd find out from other people all along. That's how she wanted it, because she was, *is*, too much of a coward to look her kids in the eye and say it—say that she cheated on Dad. With your best friend's dad, no less: Mr. .08 himself."

"So, it sounds like you won't be accompanying me for dinner at Waste-Away Shores tomorrow."

"Negative."

No use; she wasn't going to budge.

"Subject change. The debate . . ."

"Yeah, I'm running social damage control," she said. "Eric has something special planned for Mike after football practice tomorrow."

"Yay, but I also kissed Cameo today."

"That's a mistake I can't correct," she said. "Did you use protection?"

"From the sun? It didn't last long enough to catch anything," I said. "And just out of curiosity, why don't you like her?"

"She's a cock tease, Jay. Loses interest as soon as she wins a guy over. Girls like her are a dime a dozen."

Funny, that was how much I thought Cam's boyfriends were worth. That would make her relationships . . . a fair trade. Cameo was balancing out our shitty economy.

"There's more to her than that," I insisted.

Abby sighed, saying, "Maybe I'm jaded because of her dad. But all I see when I look at her is freshman skank. You can do better, dumb-ass."

The way she said "dumb-ass" . . . it was almost tender. An example of why I kept doggy-paddling back to her island. Bark bigger than her bite, my big sister protected me.

"You love me, don't you?" I said.

"Stop it. You sound like Mom."

"Aaabby," I imitated, "come see your mommy tomorrow."

"You drive a hard bargain . . . but not really."

"You cannot resist my brotherly charm."

"Good thing Lazzie and I got vaccinated yesterday."

Good time to let forth a fart noise, my lips blubbering in an approximation of a bear fart.

"Bwraarphhh."

My call of the wild sounded accurate to me. I started to sing "I Just Ripped One" as a follow-up, but it was too late. We were laughing into our pillows already.

TRACK 14

The Landslide Brought Me Down to Rock Bottom

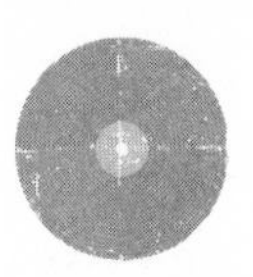

At school the next day, I kept my head down in the halls and in my books during class. Hoping to avoid Cameo. It seemed like a whole week had gone by in a day and I was starting over. I kind of was, though, in more ways than one.

Luckily, I'd found something else to do during lunch. Ms. Lambert was quick to forgive yesterday's shenanigans and said I could hang out in her room—if I helped her grade papers.

"Are you mucho excited about your date with detention tonight?" she teased. "Picture it: Jay Baker, Mr. Future Valedictorian himself, slumming it after school with all the other pseudo-rebels."

"It'll be an experience," I said confidently. "And you're always kvetching about how I should broaden my horizons, right? 'Go to Europa, Jay. Overdo it on the Old Spice and smoke cigarettes like the Euro-trash you were always meant to be.'"

"If only we could hold detention at the Louvre," she said. "*Mais non,* Coach Ellington is on duty this week, so you're about to become *even more* familiar with the wonderful world of game tape."

"How many times does he need to relive last year's zero-fourteen season? I'm just sayin'."

"Yes, poodle, if anyone can put the 'I' back in team, it's you."

I smiled. "My sister thinks we have a shot at the Homecoming Game."

"I know!" Ms. Lambert said, clapping her hands together excitedly. "Waynesfield barely has enough Tigers to take the field. Too bad Homecoming isn't until October. Ha!"

"A loss still isn't out of the question, especially if Mike Hibbard sees any playing time."

"You'll be seeing Mike in detention tonight," Ms. Lambert cautioned. "Try to exercise some self-control. I should put that on your grade card, actually . . . *needs to improve self-control.*"

She pretended to jot something down on a Post-it.

"I'll do my Boy Scout's best," I said, "provided you create a special 'fat-kid-friendly' badge of honor for me."

Ignoring that one, she said, "You know who else will be in detention?"

"Denise Richards?"

"Close. Caroline Richardson."

"So?"

"Soooo," Ms. Lambert said, "she's a nice girl. She's in my seventh-period class and would give you a run for your money in the precociously intelligent department. Has some problems with attendance because of her tennis schedule, but I suspect that's not her fault."

"Her father is a psycho," I confirmed. "I see them out on the court all the time, him feeding her ball after ball."

"And I hear him shouting through my window. 'Racket back! Racket back!' Typical man, repeating himself louder and louder to get his point across. Hello. We're listening. I don't get it."

"Caroline doesn't talk much," I said, "but with him as her ventriloquist, I can understand why. Plus, she's the new girl, and they usually don't display a personality trait for at least a year."

"So speed up the big reveal, why don't you?"

"I barely know her."

"Get to. Broaden your horizons, Jay. Dr. Doolittle's appointment book looks a little full these days. It would do you good to get out of *her* waiting room for a little while. But you didn't hear that from me."

She looked down and pretended to be busy.

"I know you're not really doing anything," I said.

"Hurry up and grade my papers."

Why was Ms. Lambert meddling in my biz? Like Abby, it almost seemed as if she was pushing me away from Cameo. A Cameo backlash was sweeping the nation. She definitely was a large cereal bowl full of frosted flakiness when it came to guys, but she'd been my friend since second grade.

As I walked to detention, I couldn't stop myself from ruminating further. No doubt, Cam was a tease. And whenever she had a new boyfriend, her texts and phone calls slowed down considerably. Then, as soon as the relationship fizzled, I was the temporary stand-in. Now we had the kiss and our parents' affair to complicate matters, and I was the one fretting while she played it cool. She made me feel like a natural woman, and as appreciative as I was of girl-on-girl action, there wasn't room for two in our particular relationship.

This mess was enough to make my Humpty-Dumpty self run into walls, which, at that exact moment, I did. A big bloated barricade named Mike Hibbard, standing right outside Mr. Ellington's door.

After I dislodged my right arm from the depths of his stomach, I recovered enough to say, "Sorry, dude."

He just stared at me, agitated. With Mr. Ellington in sight, he had to contain himself—from snorting, "Get in my belly," then trying to eat me.

Meanwhile, I was sick of playing this tired game of one-upmanship with him.

"Perhaps we should just forgive and forget, Mike," I said, sighing. "Call a truce and stop trying to make fools of each other. Isn't this whole Tom and Jerry thing getting a little old?"

He mulled over my peace offering, but then shook his head.

"Figures you'd say that," he said, "considering you're the gay little mouse in the situation."

He still wanted to go at it, which was fine, because he'd left the superior analogy for me.

"Well, considering you're such a fat, stretched-out pussy, I'd always assumed you were the cat."

Mike clenched his fists, his cheeks turning their typical wind-burned red.

"C'mon, dude," I said. "Don't get all hot and bothered about one of my harmless barbs. A little laughter might clear up your rosacea. It was a joke."

"You're a joke, *dude*," he whispered vehemently. "Since you're so gay and can't get it up for Parnell, you had to have your slut mommy go out and hump her dad for you."

I choked back my anger, trying to maintain control.

"What is wrong with you?" I said. "You know, for someone so convinced that *I'm* gay, *you* sure do bring it up a lot. Maybe you should look in the mirror tonight, as hard as that may be, and figure out why your reflection is whacking it to animal porn and eating Fiery Buffalo Doritos at the same time—"

"Get in here, you two!" Mr. Ellington barked from his desk.

So much for bygones. By golly, the feud must go on. Mike began walking into the classroom.

"While your mom watches," I whispered behind him.

Had to make sure I got that in.

TRACK 15

Muskrat Love Will Keep Us Together (in Detention)

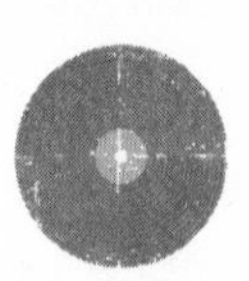

Sure enough, as Ms. Lambert had forecast, I spotted Caroline in the back of Mr. Ellington's classroom. She really wasn't a detention kind of girl. Seemed too efficient—like she was going through life point by point—to stop, sit, and do nothing. Drumming her fingers on her desk, her chin resting on her palm, she looked more than a little on edge. Maybe we *did* have a lot in common.

She saw me and smiled her perfect smile—not quite showing all her teeth this time. I took a seat next to her in the back, trying and probably failing to appear like a guy with cool things on his mind.

"No talking, no food or drinks, one bathroom break," Mr. Ellington said to the eight people in the room. "Otherwise, I don't care what you do."

He gestured for Mike to join him by the television for some

game-tape viewing, and I resisted the urge to cough "lost cause" into my arm.

To my right, I noticed Caroline staring out the window at something. Her hair was up in a no-nonsense bun, every strand in place. Her face was makeup-free, but her skin was tanned, olive, and beautiful; she didn't need any of that powdery nastiness the other girls in school *Proactive*ly overused to hide their blemishes. Her nose, from this angle, looked otherworldly in its perfection, sculpted by Michelangelo after he'd finished painting all those naked angels on the Sistine Chapel. The slope was straight and strong, the bridge extending from her face in just the right place. She had her usual T-shirt and sweats on—her twiggy body comfortably swimming in both—and appeared ready to drop and give her dad twenty on command.

I just gawked at her beautiliciousness. Blinded by Cameo and her feminine wiles for so long, the change of scenery was eye-opening.

Caroline had a definite aura about her. She glowed. And, for an hour and a half at least, she was all mine.

I took out a piece of paper and pen and started writing my little detention-trapped glowworm a note.

"What are you staring at?" I wrote. "Want to know what I'm doing? No? I'm telling you, anyway. I'm staring at your arm like a creeper. I think I could fit my hand around it. Twice. Let's measure the circumference with my compass. You won't feel a thing."

I furtively placed the note on her desk. She turned around

and looked at me with her large, penetrating green peepers. *Boom.* My heart leapt; my stomach fluttered, but not in a bad, Irritable Bowel Syndrome kind of way. The butterflies weren't out to get me this time.

She wrote back, "Cheers to the skinny arm club, but point that compass toward Mike's ego. I'm staring at those two squirrels chasing each other. See them? Fascinating, eh? Ha-ha. They're kind of cute. Should I name them Chip 'n' Dale?"

I looked up from the note and she was smiling again, a certain playfulness outlining the corners of her lips.

I wrote, "Weren't they chipmunks? Regardless, can they *rescue ranger* us away from detention? Anyway, stare this way, C-line, if what you're really interested in is cuteness. I must know, Ms. Tennis-bot, why are you here? Shouldn't you be hitting a basket of balls right now?"

I passed her the note and shook my head imperceptibly. If Ms. Lambert could see me now, making the best out of a bad situation.

Her response: "Ahhhh, chipmunks. Oops! Dad couldn't convince Vice Principal Sanders to excuse the five tardies I've accumulated in the three weeks since school started. The school is willing to be flexible with my tournament schedule because there's no official tennis team, but Dad pushes them to their limit. He's a pusher. So they're hitting him where it counts and interrupting my after-school tennis practice with detention. He's furious. Oh, no, sorry this is so long and boring. And I do think you're cute, BTW. ☺"

Caroline was so talented that her dad refused to let her play with any of the predominantly male onlookers who stopped to watch her practice. She was nationally ranked, and he hauled her around from tournament to tournament and . . . wait just a second. Did she just jot down that I was cute? I wasn't used to that kind of direct approach. Check that, homie, I wasn't used to girls calling me cute. Didn't she want to play a few mind games first? Some Playboy Bunny–approved cerebral hopscotch? Flirt with me, then turn around and go out with Wade Pierson?

I stared at Caroline, who appeared not the slightest bit embarrassed by her admission. "Reversal," she seemed to say. "Skip me, back to you." Uno! I was the only self-conscious one.

I started scrawling quickly: "Thanks. Like a manorexic version of the Gossip Girl guy with man-bangs, I hear. The ladies can't resist. They're powerless against my supple bones, and I love to MILK it for all it's worth."

Self-deprecation did an unimpressive body good, but Caroline didn't fall for my method of deflection.

"You're not very good at accepting compliments, are you? It's okay to give yourself credit for something if it's true. And sometimes even if it's not. BTW, how are you? I saw the debate . . . I'm going out on a skinny-girl limb, but I'm guessing it could have gone better for you."

I drew a traditional hangman picture underneath her last graph, made a series of dashes for the letters, and then wrote "CHOKE-JOB" above them.

My accompanying response: "I'm fine. A little humiliated, but I'll get over it. It's not anything people haven't heard before from Mike. He has his group of friends; I have my laptop. As far as the election goes, I never cared that much about being class president."

"You didn't? I thought you were really into student government??"

"That's embarrassing."

"Ha-ha. If not, then what do you care about? What's your thing?"

"I have no idea," I wrote. "Maybe you can help me. Be my mentor, and I'll glean the meaning of life from you. Tell me what it is that YOU care about."

She stared at the paper in concentration. The delicate skin around her eyes crinkled just a little bit when she was thinking. Could she tell the word "glean" had a sexual connotation?

She wrote a few sentences and passed the note back.

"I care about being happy. And the people I love being happy. It's hard to ask for anything more than that. If I do, that's when I run into trouble. Maybe you're asking too much of yourself, Jay. Or of other people? I don't know. . . . ☺"

I smiled at her, then wrote, "I've always asked a lot of myself, and I use that as justification for asking the same of others. It's a philosophy that's worked out terribly, so I just might steal yours. Are you happy?"

"Happy enough, all things considered. This is depressing. It's like we're co-writing a suicide letter. Subject change! Hey, my dad told me to work on serves only today. He scheduled a conference call since we can't practice as long because of detention. Do you want to come over to the courts after we're released?"

Tonight was the dinner at Holiday Shores. I wasn't sure if

Mom knew that *I knew.* And she had no idea I was in detention right now. Fibbing was infinitely easier to do via text, and I'd sent her a doozy last night: "Helping out with a canned goods drive . . . pick me up at 4:30, please." I snaked my phone out of my pocket and texted her another: "Found a ride, be a little late." My "ride" was make-believe, but I'd worry about that later.

I wrote back to C-line: "Who, me? I'd love to. I used to play on weekends with my parents. Even had a few years' worth of lessons back in the simpler days of middle school when they still had hope for me, athletically. Beware of my, as they put it, 'natural hand-eye coordination.' It could be the end of you feeling satisfied with yourself."

In lieu of writing, she whispered, "I'll chance it."

TRACK 16

Pretty-Sweet Symphony (in eHarmony)

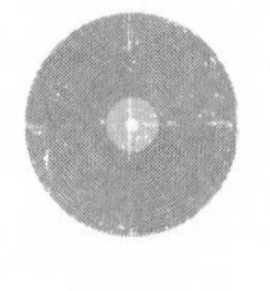

I had my gym clothes with me, so after detention I slipped into the boys' restroom and changed for my court date with Caroline. I checked myself out in the dirty mirror, all arms, legs, and a giant floating head that looked ready to join the Macy's Thanksgiving Day Parade. I needed something else: a muscle or two, or perhaps a Björn Borg headband.

I walked out to the courts—built during the late-seventies tennis boom, but abandoned in the mid-eighties when fun-eraser Ivan Lendl crashed the party, won all the trophies, and left with the ILHS team's budget. Caroline was there, already working diligently on her serve. She had a basket of balls by her side, orange target cones placed in the service box of the opposite end of the court. I watched her take three balls from the basket, conceal them in various places on her personage—hidden locales I wanted to discover—and then fire away. She obliterated two cones, narrowly missing the third.

Caroline's serve was fluid, her body languid as she set up, pushed off, and extended her racket toward the ball at its apex. Her motion possessed none of the hitches that haunted pretty much every middling tennis player who'd ever played the game, including me. She looked like a professional, and at that moment, I became determined not to unveil *my* USTA-unapproved serve. Hell, at that second, I officially had a crush. There was something so attractive about watching a girl do her thang so well, especially when she wasn't aware she had an audience. Cameo who? I wanted more of this cuteness. And if that was the wrong decision, then for once I didn't want to be right.

Caroline turned around and saw me standing behind the fence watching her.

"Hey!" she called out. "C'mere, you. You're not a spectator today."

"Oh, all right," I said, opening the door through the fence. "I guess I'll show you how it isn't done."

She handed me one of her extra rackets and pointed toward the opposite side of the court.

"You. There. Go on with your bad self, Grasshopper. I need to hit ground strokes for a little bit. My shoulder hurts."

I trotted over to the other end, attempting to look as agile as possible. I turned around and caught her smiling at me, then nearly ran into the net post—swerving out of the way at the last second.

"Did you see that?" I called out.

"Yes!" she cried, laughing.

I went all the way back to the baseline, but she shook her

head and beckoned me forward to the service line, where she was standing. "We'll start up here," she said. "Mini tennis. So we can warm up and concentrate on our form."

Caroline fed the ball my way; I met it far too late and sent it careering toward her head. She easily volleyed it out of the air and it bounced back perfectly into my box—ready for me to flail away again.

"Shorten your backswing," she instructed.

My second shot landed at her feet, barely touching the ground before she scooped it up and redirected it to the exact same spot.

"You need to get your racket back sooner," she said, smiling.

I did. And my next shot was much better. We hit back and forth that way for a while, then she waved me back to the baseline and restarted the rally from there. Little by little, the rhythm of the game came back to me. And it was sort of mesmerizing. Hitting the stupid yellow ball required all my attention; otherwise, I'd send it flying into the fence and be forced to smile like an idiot who didn't know his own strength. Well, the strength of Caroline's fancy racket.

Caroline walked up to the net, motioning for me to join her. Once there, she grabbed my right hand—still holding the racket—and inspected where my fingers were clasping the grip.

"Relax," she said. "Jeez, are you always this high-strung?"

"Pretty much."

"You could break a string without even hitting the ball."

I laughed as she began loosening my index finger with hers.

"There," she said gently, still touching me. "That's a start. Poor guy. You looked like you were in pain."

"I was."

And now the hairs on the back of my neck were at attention. Lord, couldn't I be touched (by an angel) without bristling like Sonic the Hedgehog?

"Your forehand grip keeps sliding from a semi-Western to Continental," she said, letting go of my hand. "Keep checking. Whenever you feel it slipping, put your racket flat on the ground and pick it back up. That's where your fingers should be."

"You should post an instructional video on YouTube," I said, trying to look boldly into her green eyes.

"Let's see if this works first," she said.

It did. When we resumed rallying, the racket felt far more comfortable in my hand.

I called out, "We've been hitting for ten minutes and I feel like I owe you money."

"No payment required yet," she said. "I want to win your tiddlywinks fair and square. We'll play a drop-hit game from the baseline. Feed the ball in with a ground stroke and play out the point. First person to ten wins a dollar."

"Before you clean me out of house and soda, I need a Mountain Dew," I said, pointing to the pop machine in the distance.

"No, you don't."

I'd settle for the chance to Mountain Dew her someday. (Saw that on a T-shirt once.)

An hour and a half later, we were sitting against the fence. No beverage to call my own, not to mention the fact that I now owed her ten dollars, we both drank out of Caroline's gigundo water thermos.

"Let's play a drinking game," she said.

"I tried some of my dad's Crown Royal once and lost my will to live."

"With water," she clarified. "Every time we take a drink, we have to tell the other person something no one else at school knows."

This could only lead to trouble.

"Sounds like TMI waiting to happen," I said skeptically. "You really are a sadist, aren't you? First you make my legs feel like tree trunks, and now you're digging for awkward seeds. Why don't we just fart in front of each other and call it even?"

Did I just say "fart" in front of this girl?

I continued on, hoping she didn't notice: "And how do I know Mike Hibbard didn't hire you? That you won't blog about this or something? Everyone has a blog these days and—"

"Shhh . . . calm yourself, Grasshopper. It doesn't have to be your deepest, darkest secret. Just something interesting. And I don't have any friends yet, so you're safe."

"You first," I said quickly.

"Okay," she said, taking a swig. "I hate tennis. Correction: I hate the monotony of tennis. This is the first time I've enjoyed myself on the court in a long time."

"Because of your dad?"

"No commenting afterward," she said, smiling mischievously. "Go."

"I've had a pathetic crush on my best friend for eight, maybe nine years, and now I'm not sure if she's the girl I thought she was."

"I've been wondering what's up with you two," she said.

"No comments."

"Oops, my bad," she said. "Okay, I'm half Filipino—on my mom's side—but you can't really tell I'm Asian, can you?"

"No comment," I said, even though I could tell. There was something exotic about Caroline. She didn't look like other girls.

"Touché," she said. "Go."

"I just found out my mom is fornicating with Cameo's dad."

"Good one!" she said, then caught herself. "Oh, gosh, I meant in the context of the game. . . ."

"I know," I said, smiling.

"No, but I'm sorry. Maybe this wasn't such a good idea."

"You're not giving up, are you?" I teased.

She grabbed the bottle from me.

"Unfortunately, I have a topper," she said, a dash of melancholia to her voice now. "I called this a drinking game to be ironic. My mom is an alcoholic who's been to rehab three times and has since moved back to the Philippines with my grandmother because my father says she can't be trusted. And I happen to agree with him. That's why I moved here. Fresh start."

Did she really just tell me that? If the brisk air around us wasn't loaded before, it was now.

"You win."

"Yes, I think I do," she said, readjusting her tennis bun. "But yours is pretty bad, too."

She gave me the bottle back, and I drank deeply.

"I'm sorry about your mom, Caroline."

"It's okay," she said. "Quick, your turn, before I get sad about it."

"I don't want you to think I'm saying this because I owe you something," I said, "but this is the most fun I've had in . . . I don't know how long. You. The tennis. We should do something else sometime."

And in what car would I be picking her up? Would I be getting my license six months early? Enlisting the services of Dr. Eliza Doolittle?

"Sure," she agreed.

"Nice," I said, happily pushing off the minor details until later.

"Hey, my dad is pulling in," she said. "Do you want to stop by tomorrow after he and I practice? I can probably convince him to hang around so we can hit for a little while. . . ."

"That sounds stellar," I said. "Stellar Artois."

"Huh?"

"Never mind."

"Oh, did you mean the beer? That's kind of funny."

"Never mind," I said again.

"Hey, do you have a ride?" she asked.

"Yep, Mom will be here any minute," I lied. I didn't want to ride in a car with Caroline's creepy dad. I could feel him glaring at me from the parking lot, probably wondering how I'd deprogrammed his tennis-bot to stop serving.

"Okay, then. See you tomorrow."

She smiled at me and held out her hand, palm up. I stood there and looked into her expectant green eyes. What did she want me to do? Give her a low five?

"Ooooh," I said, "you want your money."

"No, I want your hand."

I gave it to her, and she squeezed. It pretty much felt like the best thing ever.

TRACK 17

REUNITED AND IT FEELS SO AWKWARD

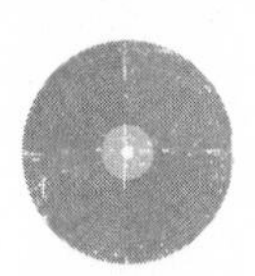

After Caroline and her dad drove away, I looked at my cell and saw four missed calls from Mom. I pressed the send button and she answered on the first ring.

"Jay?" she said, sounding both frustrated and relieved.

"No, it's Donny Osmond, your favorite crooner. If I'm a little bit rock and roll, then that would make you a little bit—"

"Worried, Jay. What's going on? I got your text, but you didn't say *who* was giving you a ride."

"An environmentally conscious sophomore ran out of room in her smart car."

"Even if that's true, it isn't like you to miss my calls. Can I come get you now? Should I bring by some canned goods?"

"Yes, I'm ready, but leave the yams at home. We'll talk when you get here."

"Are you staying the night tonight?" she asked hopefully.

Why was I doing this again? Attempting to have the Some

Dude Named Keith conversation alone? What was the point? Inevitably, I would lose my nerve and fail to hold Mom accountable. Thanks again, Abby. She'd been saddling me with each and every Mombligation since we were kids: "You're the one who likes her, Jay!"

"I don't have any clothes," I said. "And I have to feed Buffy. Who knows when Dad and Abby will be home?"

"We can stop by the house on our way," she said. "I want to see my dog. Make sure she's getting enough rest, ha-ha."

To hurt or not to hurt her by rejecting the overnight invitation—that was the mother-f'ing question.

"She claims to have mono, but I think she's just trying to skip obedience school," I said, sighing. "Sure, I'll stay. Are you coming, or should I hitch a ride with Ezekiel and this Amish buggy trotting down the road?"

"I'm already on my way, Buckwheat."

Trying to keep the car ride with Mom conversation-free, I searched the radio for anything other than a song by the Black Eyed Peas—divine musical payback for my "canned-goods cover story." Every time I turned up the volume, though, Mom would turn it down, intent on asking me questions about my day. Her persistence was extremely annoying, but understandable on a more rational level. A level at which I wasn't operating.

"Now, *where* is the school delivering the canned goods, bud?" she asked for the second time.

Fed up, I decided to be honest: "Timbuktu, Mom. There wasn't a food drive. I was in detention."

"Detention?!" she cried. "My perfect son? What in the world for?"

"I shat myself and refused to clean it up."

"Do you always have to rely on sarcasm? I'm not going to feed you until you say something earnest."

"The debate went poorly yesterday."

"Why?"

"Why do you think, Mom?"

"I really don't know, Jay," she said, lips pursed. "That's why I'm asking."

"I was a little distracted over the weekend," I said pointedly. "I came in unprepared, undercooked. But it's okay. No big deal. I'm way too socially awkward to be anyone's president. I probably would have assassinated myself out of frustration."

"But it's all you've talked about."

"I'm trying to move on," I said, first thinking of Cameo, then Caroline.

"Okay, honey, help me out here," Mom said, ignoring me. "I'm not mad that you got a detention. I'm just trying to understand what happened."

I groaned impatiently. "It all started with the birth of Mike Hibbard."

"Him again?"

"Yeah."

"You boys used to be such good friends."

"There was a scene at the debate. We both said some things we shouldn't have, and I got into it with Ms. Lambert afterward. That's the whole kit 'n' caboodle. Not very interesting, but yeah . . ."

I conveniently lip-glossed over the school-skipping make-out session with Cameo—held at Mom's house.

"Oh, Jay. I'm sorry it didn't work out." She patted my arm, then ran her hand through her thick blond hair again and again, finally deciding to utilize her signature Ray-Ban aviator sunglasses (she had ten pairs) as a headband to keep it out of her face. She grabbed another pair from the glove compartment and put those on, too. She looked at me and smiled, and I struggled not to laugh.

"Aw, you're so serious," she said. "This whole thing with your dad and me is affecting you, right? I hate that we're having such a negative impact on your life."

"It is what it is, Mom."

"I've never understood what that meant."

"Confusing, isn't it? Trying to figure out why people say the things they say, do the things they do."

She pulled into our driveway, and I hopped out to grab some clothes. Mom waited in the car.

"You're not coming in?" I asked.

"I don't think so," she said, tellingly. "Will you let Buffy out so I can see her?"

I guess it was just Dad's house now, I thought, opening the front door. The dog, alert for once, bounded out toward Mom's SUV.

Even Sleeping Buffy missed her damn mom.

TRACK 18

McOdor to My Family

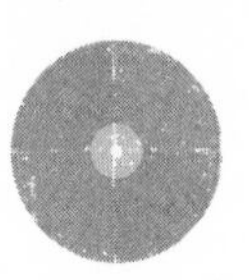

Bag packed and dog fed, Mom and I prepared to submerge our bodies in Holiday Shores. When we pulled out of the driveway, however, she turned in the direction opposite the trailer park.

"Where are we going?" I asked.

"I could use a number three from McDonald's," she said.

"Quarter Pounder plain with cheese?"

"Absolutely," she said, pushing the play button on her CD player—the Eagles began singing "Hotel California."

"I'll be having mine without."

"Of course you will," she said. "My son, the salt-burger eater."

"You're one to talk, putting that little pillar of sodium in the corner of your plate to dip your fries in."

"It's nice having the option there," she said, laughing.

How many trips to McDonald's had we made together in the course of fifteen years?

"I definitely inherited your eating habits, Mom," I said, smiling. "Don't you feel just a tad bit guilty about that?"

My stomach turned over as the word "guilty" hung in the air.

"I'm a parent, Jay," she replied. "I have guilt that goes on for miles. The pollution of my life."

"An appropriate metaphor as you drive this tank down the road," I said.

"I like being up high," she said. "It makes me feel safe."

"You could level the Hotel California going twenty."

But would she be "getting a room" there indefinitely? For now, anyway, I was her passenger-side alibi.

"Do you want to eat at the bike path?" Mom asked as we flew through the Golden Arches, burgers in hand.

"Sure."

Located a mile down the road, the bike path parking lot was Mom's favorite place to dine. It overlooked the waters of Indian Lake and doubled as a McCafé for geese. *Dear PETA: I like animals, but is there a creature more entitled and less deserving than the goose?* I threw a ketchup packet at myself in response while Mom parked the SUV.

We were quiet for a little while, staring out at the lake. With the windows rolled up, only the sounds of our fry noshing could be heard over the whir of the heater (on in September because Mom was permanently freezing).

In spite of myself, I kind of wanted to talk now. "Mom . . ."

But she preempted me. "Jay, I cheated on your dad."

Not a fan of uncomfortable silence—any silence, for that matter—Mom beat me to the punch. There was no wondering from whom I'd learned the *banzai!* approach.

"With Cameo's dad, Keith," she continued, first starting to cry and then laughing at the absurdity of what she was saying. "Isn't that ridiculous? But Keith understands why . . . never mind. That's not really important."

She exhaled audibly.

"I'm not making any excuses. I know you know. Your dad called me, and gosh, I should've told you sooner. This whole . . . ordeal . . . has gotten away from me. Even though I'm supposed to be the adult, the mother, I feel like a kid again. Makes me miss my mom more than ever," she said, sliding my grandma's wedding ring back and forth along her necklace. "This is all new, and I keep making mistakes. I'm so sorry."

It was surreal to see my doting mother being so un-mom-like. She was forcing me to step outside of our relationship and view her from a different perspective, which wasn't easy. Why shouldn't I hold her to a higher standard than everyone else? Wait, why should I? I kept going back and forth.

"I guess I don't understand why you've done this . . . or why you keep doing this, Mom."

She grabbed a tissue from her purse and blew her nose.

"I'm not making excuses," she said again, "but your dad, Jay. Well, he said he'd cut back on his hours when he got promoted a few years ago, but then he started working more than ever. We used to fish in tournaments, take trips, go on actual dates together. Somewhere along the line, we stopped doing any of that. We lost something. Then the Keith thing just kind of . . . happened."

"Shit happens," I said. "*Keith* was your choice."

"I know," she said carefully. "You're right. But I'm just saying this isn't something I went actively searching for. When you feel abandoned by someone, I guess . . . well, maybe I was searching and didn't even realize it."

I rolled down the window and threw the rest of my bun toward the geese.

"So what now?" I asked. "Are you still on the prowl? Have you found what you're looking for in Keith Parnell? Where does Dad fit in? What's the deal, Mom?"

"I don't know yet," she said. "Your dad . . . he's a very proud man. He'll probably never get past my mistake to see that he plays a part in all this."

"You're saying he's partially to blame?"

"Not for the situation with Keith," she said. "For the problems in our marriage? Yes. In my opinion, he hasn't been an equal partner for a long time."

"I read his Love Fax, Mom. The one in your jewelry box. It sounded like Dad was fifty-fifty a month ago."

Mom looked both surprised and indignant. "You went through my personal things?"

"Probably not the best moment for you to talk about your privacy, Mom."

She started to say something else, then seemed to think the better of it.

"How *did* you find the letter, surrounded by all that junk?" Mom asked, in spite of herself.

"I didn't. Cameo did. She probably saw it on *Hoarders*."

"Jay," Mom said softly, "your dad's a smart man. He knew I wanted more from him long before he wrote that."

"But why didn't you give him another chance before . . . you know . . ."

"I was exhausted from competing with his work," she said. "Your father's a great provider, but it's never enough with him. I'm not sure you understand what it's like trying to get the attention of someone who doesn't even know you're there."

Had I mentioned the name Cameo recently?

"I'm pretty sure I do, Mom," I said. "Maybe you should have talked to me about it."

"I don't know why I didn't," she said, putting the car in gear. "You've always been there for me, Jay."

When we pulled into Holiday Shores ten minutes later, there was a van parked curbside in front of Mom's trailer. The block-lettered graphic on the side of it read ".08? Need A Lift?"

"You've got to be kidding me, Mom."

"Oh, nooo!" she exclaimed.

Some Dude Named Keith Parnell was inside.

TRACK 19

Give Me One Reason Not to Shoot Myself in the Face

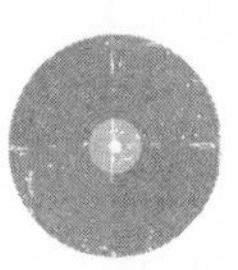

The least Keith could have done was driven a different vehicle. His rust-bucket van wasn't fit to take a dump in, and the last thing our family needed was for it to be parked outside Mom's—a flashing sign to the world that he was Magna-Doodling her on a regular basis.

Mom looked positively mortified. She took off her sunglasses and started running her fingers through her hair, struggling both internally and externally with what to do next. Always with the hair: Abby and I were exactly the same. One of her favorite jokes—Dad's, too—was when she arranged her thick blond mane in front of her face, placed her Ray-Bans over the top of it, and walked around impersonating Cousin Itt, snapping her fingers twice after "na-na-na-nah."

"I must have forgotten to tell him you were coming over tonight," she said. "I'm so sorry, Jay. We can leave."

"And go where? His house? Chuck E. Cheese's? We

already ate, my show is on in a few hours, and I hate to be the one to tell you this, but he's probably not going anywhere."

Unless there was an emergency drink-and-drive at the Thirsty Turtle, Brothers, or Desperado's—just a few of Indian Lake's many watering holes.

"You're right," she said. "Let me call him. We'll do a loop and he'll be gone. Poof, never happened."

Mom was scrolling through the numbers of her cell and edging away from the trailer when Keith came barreling out of the Florida room door, hands waving in an enthusiastic greeting. "Stop!" his lips appeared to say. "Stop!"

For what? Was he drunk? Did he think he was stranded on a deserted island? Surely this was one SOS karma would forgive us for ignoring.

Something beyond mortification befell Mom's pretty face—horror. A crease of worry appeared between her light eyebrows as she reluctantly waved back at Keith.

I stared at him. Couldn't help it. Even though he was one of Cameo's disposable parents, I hadn't seen him in a long time. Cam and I rarely hung out at her house, unless he wasn't home and her mom had ingested enough Mother's Little Helpers to last her through the night. Keith rarely attended Cameo's cheerleading functions—we had that in common—and I was too young to be gettin' tipsy at the Turtle.

The dude was a sight for the eyes, but not for the sore kind. More like the bloodshot. A good twenty pounds overweight, he wore denim nut-huggers way too tight for his meaty thighs and a flannel button-down shirt with no T-shirt underneath, exposing copious amounts of not-so-distinguished salt-and-pepper chest hair. The coif on his head hung down past his ears; three days of stubble made his face look strangely darker than it should. He was quite the Chi-chi-chia display, a forty-something pet sold at your local Wrong Aid. It was as if his sole purpose was to remind people he was still capable of hair growth.

Being alone seemed like a much better alternative to being with this guy, but obviously Mom didn't think so. Flabbergasted, I turned to her, and she could barely meet my gaze.

"He won't stay long," she promised, pulling into the carport.

"That's comforting."

We stepped out of the car. Keith waited for us by the door, still smiling.

"Hi, pie!" Keith said. "Good to see you, Jay! How are you guys? Wasn't expecting *both* y'all tonight."

"A round of surprises for everyone," I said. Then I caught the look of dread in Mom's eyes and forced myself to say, "Nice to see you, too. *Keith.*"

Barely got out that "Keith." Was "pie" his nickname for Mom? As in . . . honey pie? Sugar pie? American pie? And what was with the "y'all"? We lived in Ohio. Only Ms. Lambert could get away with that.

"Hey, Keith," Mom said, walking toward him. They hugged quickly. It was briefly obnoxious.

We headed into the trailer. Once I stepped over the threshold, I felt like one of the three bears—forced to hang out with two-timing Goldilocks and her sketchy boy on the side, who also happened to be my best friend's father. Immediately, I noticed Keith's "work" boots on *my* footstool, which meant he'd been sitting in *my* chair, watching *my* plasma, with a bottle of beer on the coaster where *my* Mountain Dew should have been.

I must have been fixating on the area, because Keith's eyes followed the direction of mine. He hurried over to clean up his mess. He placed his boots against the wall, grabbed for the beer, and promptly knocked it over onto the carpet.

"Awww, shit!" he cried.

He grabbed the bottle, the foamy contents still spilling out, and hurried into the kitchen saying, "Sorry! Sorry, pie!"

When Keith came back with a dirty towel, Mom gently took it from his hand, carrying it into the kitchen. "Let's trade this for a clean one," she said, laughing a little. I'd botched enough Mountain Dew quench sessions to know Mom was cool with spills on her Berber.

"Looks like ol' Keith-a-rino had an accident," Keith said, trying to regain his composure. "You're never too old to spill a beer, are you, Jay?"

"I wouldn't really know—"

"Just joshin' you, Jaybird," he said, walking over to me. "I know you're a good egg. Cam always says so."

Inches from my face—a space-invading close talker of the

beer-breath kind—he held out his hand. When I didn't take it right away, he made a chopping motion with his fingers.

I really didn't want to give Keith the satisfaction of thinking his presence here was copacetic, but he waited me out. I extended my hand and clasped his. I almost opted for the dead fish, but then I squeezed his palm at the last second.

"It's really good to see you, Jay," he said, smiling.

His teeth were surprisingly white, and belatedly I recognized some vestige of handsomeness underneath his forty-three sheets to the wind, Dennis Quaid–like veneer. A man worthy of seducing my mother underneath my roof-over-head-providing father's nose? That was another story.

"Yeah," I said. "Same."

Since this Neander-drawler was such a fan of sign language, I threw in a sarcastic thumbs-up sign—as if I knew any other way to convey the gesture. I had a few other choice gestures up my sleeve, too, if he stuck around for much longer.

"Your mom didn't tell me you were coming over tonight," Keith said, shifting his weight and finally stepping back. "I would've picked up a pizza from Eddie's or something."

Located near Whereabouts Town, Eddie's was local bar pizza, of course. For the record, their pizza was disgusting. Mom had brought it home a few times, possibly after letting Keith add an ingredient to her pie.

Mom returned with a wet towel and some of that magic spray she was amazed you could buy for a Sacagawea at Dollar General.

"We already ate, Keith," she said, leaning down to spray

and wipe the carpet. "And Jay's on an Amore's kick. He'll only order from there these days."

"He's a teenager, pie," Keith persisted. "He'll eat anything. You won't even try Eddie's, Jay?"

I was starting to feel an increasingly familiar tension in the back of my neck; the room now seemed oppressively warm. This was too overwhelming.

"It's sort of a love affair I've got going on with Amore's, Keith," I said. "I'd feel like I was *cheating* on them if I ordered from somewhere else. I'm sure you can understand."

Mom and Keith both froze.

Ah, there he was: my born-again inner snarkster delivering that little fetus to their doorstep. It's a boy! Sorry, but someone had to throw these two a cold shower and show them their actions bred consequences.

"Sure, I gotcha," Keith said, recovering quicker. "That'd be like me switching to Coors outta nowhere. Or your mom switching brands of those nasty ciggies she used to swear by. . . ."

"Used to?" I said, looking at Mom inquisitively.

"I quit," Mom said, adjusting her black knit shrug. "Started myself on the Nicorette program, and the gum tastes about like cancer would. I've wanted to stop forever, but I couldn't convince your dad. The only time we were spending together was in the garage, so . . . anyway. Keith is helping me."

"That I am," said Keith.

Oh, how cute. Keith Parnell, a Surgeon's General Warning in his own right, was worrying about Mom's health. This wasn't some passing fling! I'd stumbled upon a love to last a lifetime.

"Yeah, Keith," I began, ready to deliver again. But then I looked at Mom—so desperate for me to be civil—and I couldn't declare the war.

"I have to go sink a few battleships in the bathroom," I said.

"Down the hall to your left, Skipper," Keith said.

"Thanks for the directions, Captain Obvious."

TRACK 20

I Just Called to Say I'm Pooping

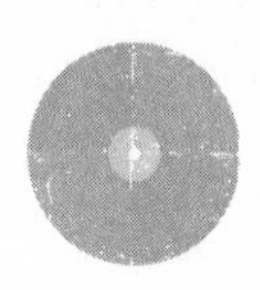

Safely in the bathroom, I lifted the toilet's carpet-covered lid—the carpet matched the drapes, in this instance—and dropped my pants. I sat down and called my sister, sick of playing house with the two lovebirds by my lonesome (dove).

"Hello?"

She actually answered.

"Is Abby there?"

"This is Abby, how can I help you?"

"I have an emergency Some Dude Named Keith situation," I said.

"Huh?"

"I need a Keith-endectomy."

"Use your big-kid words, Jay."

"Keith's fracking over here, Abby," I whispered. "His van was parked out front when we pulled in, and then he ambushed us before we could drive away. Now I'm trapped and Mom doesn't seem in any hurry to make him leave. And you were supposed to be here. And, finally, I hate you."

She sighed, telling her background noise (Eric) to shut up.

"She's something else, our madre. Want me to pick you up?"

I thought about that for a second.

"No," I said.

"Why?"

"I dunno . . . I don't feel like wiping down the crime scene."

At this point, I didn't even feel like wiping my ass.

"Are you pooping?" she asked. "I just heard something suspicious."

"Maybe."

Abby sighed again. "Who cares if you hurt Mom's feelings, Jay? She's the one giving you the IBS attack, not the other way around. You have to quit letting her walk all over you and—"

"Okay, okay, slow down," I interrupted. "I let you walk over me all the time."

"That's different," she said. "I'm your beautiful, all-knowing sister and your future Homecoming Queen. Found out this afternoon, and it will be announced tomorrow."

"Congratulations," I said. "Now you can wear a crown while giving Eric the royal treatment. But wait, are you sure he'll still know it's you?"

"Shut up."

"Make me."

"Look, Jay, I've gotta go. You know I hate talking on the phone. Text if you want me to pick you up."

"Text this," I said.

"No, text this," she said.

"Suck my texticular."

Laughing, she hung up.

Thirty minutes later, I was no longer in labor and was sitting at the dinner table, hungry for my second course of the night. While I'd been in the bathroom, Mom had ordered pizza, after all.

"The last thing your stomach needs is more greasy food, Jay," she said, placing the Amore's box on the table. "But as long as you think you're okay."

"Never better."

Dammit. The pizza box was closer to Keith than me. He opened it up and selected what would have been my slice of choice—the one with the superlative dough bubble on it.

Mom's eyes flashed to Keith's plate in despair. She knew.

"Keith, wait," she said, taking the piece from his plate and placing it on mine. "This one has less grease on it. Jay should eat it."

"No problemo," Keith said, selecting another.

The piece was art—the cheese high enough on the crust so that the sauce wasn't showing. I took an appreciative bite.

"Have you talked to Cameo lately, Jay?" Keith asked.

"No," I said, chewing. "Have *you?*"

Asked that a tad more viciously than I'd intended.

"Uh, no," he said, sheepish. "I can't keep up with that girl. She's like a whirlwind—a level-five tor-na-do."

He separated the syllables like Cam did sometimes: *"In-dis-cre-tion."*

"How are she and Wade?" Keith asked.

"They broke up last week," I said.

"Oh?" he said. "He seemed like a nice enough kid."

"He's not," I said. "She'll go back out with him, though. He drives a green truck with a lot of fascinating bumper stickers. You have that in common—vehicles with stuff on them."

Keith ignored the slight and turned to Mom.

"Sounds like I need to get to know this cat—eh, pie?"

Before she could respond, a pair of headlights shined brightly through the bay window. Someone had pulled into the driveway behind Mom's SUV, hitting her rubber trash can along the way.

The raven hair and olive skin of my sister were visible, barely, on the driver's side of the car. She left the engine running with the headlights on, stepped out of the vehicle, and quickly strode up the sidewalk.

TRACK 21

ICE, ICE, ABBY—TOO COLD

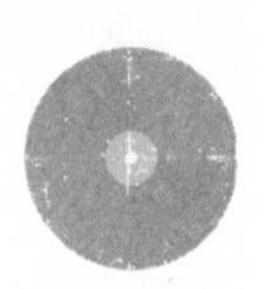

Abby flung open the door and whirled around toward the kitchen like a Tasmanian dervish. Her eyes, wild with pent-up fury, homed in on her prey: Mom. She didn't look in Keith's direction.

"Hey, Abby!" Keith said, trying to defuse the situation. "Would you like something to—"

Abby wasn't trying to hear Keith's people-appeasing bar-speak.

"Jay, let's go," she said. "Get your crap. I need you for something at home."

She'd decided to rescue me, apparently, and I was afraid to go against her.

"Okay, but I'm not brushing your hair tonight," I said. "It's demeaning."

"Abby—" Mom began.

"Mom, let's talk outside while Jay packs his bag."

Abby walked out into the Florida room, slamming the door behind her. I could hear the Maury Povich audience oohing in my head, raring to witness a surprise catfight in lieu of the customary paternity test reveal. Grab your Big Lots folding chairs; the fur was going to fly in the trailer park tonight. Chung you later, Keith, I thought, walking back to the guest room. Thank God he was *not* the father in this family.

I heard him attempt to follow the girls out. "No, Keith," Mom said firmly. "I know you're just trying to help, but I need to speak with Abby alone."

Good for Mom, facing the scary music solo. I grabbed my duffel from where I put it on the floor and noticed that she'd since turned down the bed for me. In place of a mint on my pillow, she'd folded a natty vintage airplane jacket, perfect for any danger-zone occasion. I tried it on; it fit like a bloody glove, and I was tempted to pour a glass of OJ and toast to Mom's acquittal.

Keith was sitting on the recliner messing with his cell when I returned to the living room. I actually felt some sympathy for him, alone with his Droid, not getting the reception he wanted.

"Do you have to work tonight?" I asked.

Best I could do.

"Yessir," he said. "It's a little early to hit the circuit, though."

"Uh-huh."

"Looks like the bar fight is here, anyway," he said.

"I guess," I said. "I better go out there."

"Take care, partner. Sorry if I intruded tonight. Cam always says I have the worst timing. Even when she was a little girl, I was never there when she wanted me to be."

I almost suggested that he go home and try harder, but I bit my hypocritical tongue.

"Yeah," I said, "figuring out what Cameo wants isn't an easy task for anyone. . . ."

Bag in hand, I walked out the door to find Abby and Mom already getting into it.

"Is there no limit to your selfishness, Mom?" Abby asked, haphazardly running her hands through her hair. She was standing to the far side of the room by the screen door; Mom was seated in the corner. I shut the front door softly and sat down on the top step.

"You're like a different person these days," she continued. "I guess I should have known you'd do something this inconsiderate."

"Calm down, Abby," Mom said, first pawing at the grandma rings on her necklace, then sticking almost an entire pack of Nicorette in her mouth.

"No, I won't calm down," Abby said. "You and Dad just separated, and as if it weren't bad enough that you've been cheating for however long with that *Miami Vice* reject in there, somehow you feel it's necessary to give him a key to your trailer. It's just a bad joke."

Abby sat down on one of the plastic chairs. "This whole thing couldn't get any more embarrassing. *You're* embarrassing, Mother. Honestly, do you have any idea what you're doing?"

"No," Mom said, chewing frantically. "As a matter of fact, I don't."

"Obviously."

"Can I explain?"

"The floor is yours," Abby said, waving her hand impatiently. "Say something!"

"You may think you know everything there is to know about relationships, but a marriage is far more complicated than you can ever imagine."

"I think I'm following: When times get tough, you get a divorce."

Mom had her patented sarcasm shield up: "No one said anything about divorce. A trial separation is just that. A trial. A chance for us to figure things out. We should have been clearer about that with you kids. Your dad is free to see other people, too."

"Does he really want to, though?" Abby asked. "He still loves *you*. How can you be so insensitive to that?"

"I'm not being insensitive . . . and I don't think your dad really wants—"

Abby cut her off. "Don't try to blame this on Dad. This is what you wanted, Mom."

"Please, let me finish."

"What else is there to freaking know besides the fact that you're having an affair? I know it. You know it. The entire school has known it longer than Jay and me. And now you're advertising it."

Abby pointed to the curbside .08-mobile. "Look who's

here, everyone!" she said, possessed by making her point. "And only a few days after I moved out of my husband's house!"

Abby had Mom parent-trapped, caught between being a mother and her own defense attorney.

"I didn't mean for Keith to be here tonight," Mom said, fighting back tears.

"Doesn't matter. He was. And you expect us to come visit regularly? RSVP to hang with you and Keith Parnell? FYI, I have a million other prior obligations."

"Giving Keith a key was a mistake," Mom said dejectedly. "I admit that. I'm miserable here, not being able to see you kids every day, and I'm lonely. What else do you want me to say, Abby? I'm a horrible person? I don't deserve to live?"

"Make no mistake about it, Mother," Abby said. "I don't want anything from you."

While Abby gathered her thoughts, I utilized the five seconds of silence to stop the insanity.

"Anyway. We should go, Abby. Before my IBS shows up again. We can all talk tomorrow or something."

"You're right," Abby said, standing up quickly. "My car is running, and gas isn't getting any cheaper."

Wait a second. My sister didn't care about cheap gas . . .

"Unlike our mother."

I closed my eyes. Knew she was going there.

"You still owe me ten dollars for taking you and Skankeo to the movies the other week," Abby added, walking out the screen door toward her car.

"Morning-after pill getting more expensive?" I called after her lamely.

"Hurry up!"

I wondered if she'd accept one of Keith's custom ".08? Call Keith P. or Busted!" beer cozies, a gag gift that Cameo had given me for my birthday. (I already missed our heavy-on-the-repartee rapport.)

I turned around to assess the Mom damage. She was distraught, teary-eyed, still trying to catch her breath. And I had absolutely no idea what to do or say.

"Does me in my new *Top Gun* jacket take your breath away in a good way or a bad way?" I asked.

"A great way," Mom said, laughing a little. "I knew you'd look cute in that."

She got up from her chair and stepped over to me. Her hands squeezed the sleeves of my jacket, then she hugged me tightly. Outside, the locusts sang their unpleasant song as Abby began flashing her brights in our direction.

"Don't sell yourself short, Buckwheat. You're my perfect boy. I love your sister, too, but it's never been the same with her. Even when she was a baby . . ."

Mom broke the hug and trailed off the beaten-to-death path of her familiar story.

I was *over* feeling hurt as a result of Mom's actions, but I was also *over* her being hurt. For better or worse, she was my mom.

"You know Abby, Mom. She hates everyone. Just think of yourself as part of the rule, rather than the exception. She makes none. Except for me, that is. But I'm irresistible."

"I know, honey," she said. "She's good to you. And no matter what she says, I'll always love her. Will you try to tell her that?"

"Uh, sure."

"It might help if you give her the Kate Spade I found for her at the outlet mall. Just a second." Mom ran into the house and returned a few seconds later with a woven-straw purse, handing it over to me.

"If there's one person she'll listen to, it's Kate," Mom said, forcing a smile.

"Thanks for the designer catnip," I said, arranging it underneath my arm in the most masculine way possible.

Mom stood looking out the screen door as I trotted to the car, threw my bag and "Kate Spade" into the backseat, and strapped myself into the front next to my sister's angry face and the tense body attached to it.

Abby squealed her tires out of the driveway, deliberately backing over the trash can on her way out. "Sure you don't want to throw that jacket in there before we go?" she asked.

"Was that really necessary?"

"It snuck up on me again—didn't have a choice."

"I was talking more about some of your choice words for Mom."

"What does it matter? In case it wasn't clear before, our parents' marriage is over. Mom didn't even ask Keith to leave. He just sat in there like a lawn ornament, waiting his turn. How pathetic."

"He's definitely pathetic," I agreed.

Kind of dense, too, but maybe not such a horrible guy. File that last part under things I'd never say out loud.

"Regardless of what happens, we're living with Dad," she

said, checking her rearview mirror. "Even though I really like that purse."

Abby was my big sister, we were in this together, and it was much easier to use her as a scapegoat than to make that decision myself.

"Okay," I agreed, "as long as my floor-bed rights are indefinite."

"I already made it tonight," she said.

I felt a stab of love from her direction. That's how love came from Abby—in sharp, intermittent stabs.

"No fart noises," she added.

"Pffft," I said. "Tell that to the ever-flatulent Lazzie."

"I think I love that bear more than your mother," she said.

"I've got news for you," I said. "That bear is just as big of a bed-hopper. I've slept with it many times."

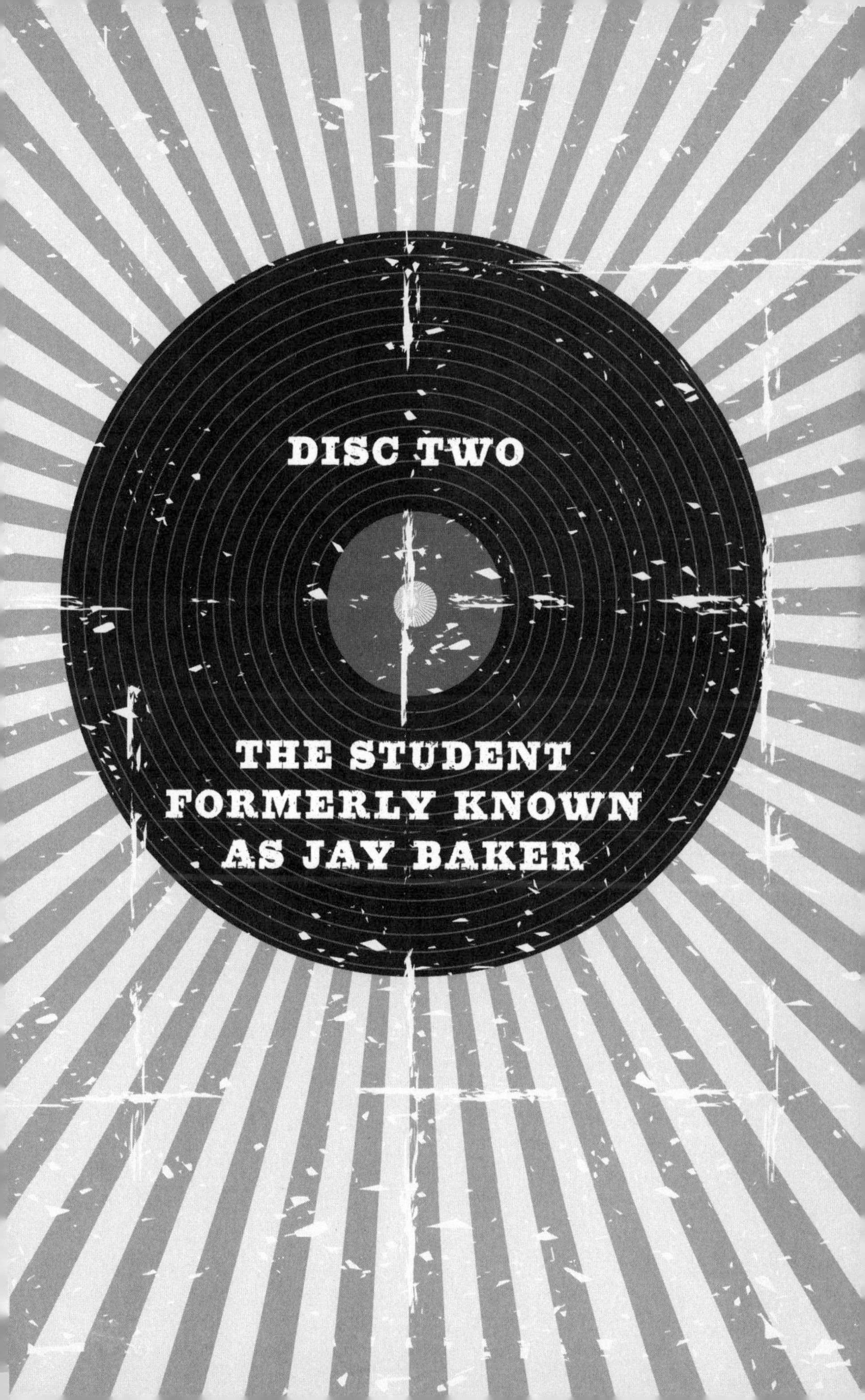
DISC TWO
THE STUDENT
FORMERLY KNOWN
AS JAY BAKER

TRACK 22

Ready or Not, a Change Is Gonna Come

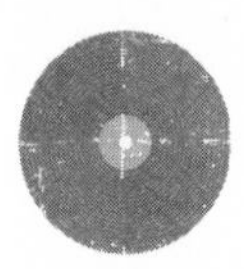

One month later

If there was one month each year the Ohio climate could be considered "tolerable"—"pretty decent" if you wanted to press your luck and risk a cold-front whammy from that fickle beyotch, Mother Nature—it was October. The temperature ranged from high sixties to low seventies, and the changing color of the leaves—from green to red to yellow to their eventual brown—gave the otherwise bleak landscape a shot of color that made shooting thyself in the face less appealing. Particularly when the sun decided to poke its fiery head out of the perma-cloudy sky.

Yes, a month had passed since the fateful day of our family meeting, but time had healed no wounds up in my piece. My home was quieter than ever; my parents more separated by the day. I missed the sight of them together so much. Alas, Dad's office chair was getting more and more tail, and Mom was working extra hours at Whereabouts Town, taking long walks on the bike path to refrain from smoking, and keeping Keith around as a really awful backup plan.

I felt partially responsible for the growing rift between Mom and Abby (a certified masseuse in the deep-tissue silent treatment). Mom hadn't stopped asking me about her. But when I made Abby sit down for dinner the other night—pizza for me, a low-calorie plate of nothing for her—she claimed to have more important agenda items to worry about than Mom's feelings. Long term: getting into Brown University. Short term: the Homecoming Game was in two weeks, the dance a day later, and she had shopping to do. She needed a celebutante-caliber frock for the dance, of course, but she also required a suit for when the Homecoming Court was introduced and escorted down the football field by their parents during halftime. When I suggested she let Mom flank her, too, she nearly Naomi Campbelled me with her cell phone. When I recommended she pick out something from Wet Slut, Forever Twenty-Cents, or White House/Same Dress, I finally netted a laugh from her on the third.

Good times. No, really, there had been a few. Just to be sure, I'd been keeping accurate records in Alba MacBook. Most of these glorified journal entries had been about Caroline, because I'd hottie-swapped. As the shared spaghetti noodle of my friendship with Cameo weakened underneath our parents' slurping, the one between Caroline and me started tasting better and better. Somehow, after umpteen reassurances from me that she wouldn't be joining a love triangle alongside Cameo, Tramp Jay had convinced Lady Caroline to be his girlfriend a week ago—October 7 to be exact. We were officially "going out," but never really going anywhere except the tennis court after school. The C-line C-blocking culprits: her dad and my crusty learner's permit.

I didn't mind my now-daily tennis hitting sessions with Caroline and her dad, especially when he worked late and she and I had the first hour of practice to ourselves. It felt good to put down the MacBook, step into the Steve Urkel transformation chamber, and emerge Stefan Urquelle. I boasted actual banana-shaped biceps now; my legs and feet felt solid beneath me. And as for my tennis skillz, well, we'd been hitting for a month and C-line said my strokes were instinctively proficient (she had no idea). "You're talented, Jay. More important, you're a competitor, a fighter. You just need to believe in yourself a little more." My ego had taken a big hit after the debate, so I was more than happy to eat her (hype) up with a spoon and stick a fork in Cameo.

Walking up to the courts after school that mid-October Monday, I spotted Caroline reading a well-known book with a red apple on the cover. Oh, no, I thought. Not her, too. Cameo had been an irreversible Twi-tard, but perhaps there was still hope for Caroline. . . .

Her hair was pulled back into her severe tennis bun, her green eyes narrowed in concentration. She looked very Asian in that moment.

"My girlfriend looks very Asian today," I said through the fence.

She turned around to face me, looking pleased. "I'll be sure to tell her."

Her face always lit up when I told her that. I think it reminded her of her mother, still exiled to the Philippines for the Green Fairy knew how long. Caroline certainly had no clue, and for the past few weeks she'd seemed far more reluctant to bring it up.

"Don't you find it a bit creepy that the plot of that shite you're reading centers 'round a century-old vampire courting a teenager?" I asked.

"Not really."

"So statutory is okay as long as the pedophile is a sexy vampire with a crooked smile?"

"Team Edward," she declared, smiling up at me. "Sounds like you've given the matter a lot of thought."

"I'm very concerned for the well-being of America's youth," I said. "Speaking of which, where's your crazy dad? I'm late. I figured I'd catch him sitting on your back reading *Authoritarianism for Dummies* while you did push-ups."

"He left for now because he's angry with my forehand," she explained. "For real. That's what he said: *I'm not mad at you, Caroline. I'm mad at your forehand.*"

I stepped inside and sat down next to her. I kissed her lips, catching a whiff of her scent: mint soap and sunscreen.

"Your forehand is perfect," I said, pressing my nose against her arm and sniffing a few more times for good measure.

She laughed. "I kept following through over my head, like Sharapova. He said he couldn't endorse such banal mimicry."

"Even with all her endorsements?"

"Very funny."

"You should spike his Gatorade with a chill pill while he's preparing your daily food pellet," I suggested.

She flashed her white teeth and kissed me. It was always better when she initiated it—felt like I'd earned something.

C-line started to pull her lips away. "My lady doth protest?" I said.

"My dad could be here any minute. Let's stick to tennis for now, Shakespeare."

"Fine, Bella. But I'm taking your 'for now' as a verbally binding rain check."

I stood up and took a couple awkward practice swings with her racket. "How do I get more topspin on my shots, like Rafael Nadal?" I asked.

"Brush underneath the ball more, then follow through around your head like I was earlier," she said. "It will complement your consistency and drive my dad to dr— I probably shouldn't finish that sentence."

"Will you come over to my house for dinner tonight?" I asked, quickly changing the subject. "I'm making Jay's Famous Spaghetti."

"You're cooking?" she asked.

We stood, took our corresponding sides of the court, and began rallying back and forth from the service line.

"Don't sound so surprised," I said. "I told Dad I'd make dinner for this chick Alice since we owe her."

"Who's Alice?"

"A friend of my aunt's," I explained. "She started bringing by rancid casseroles a few weeks ago in exchange for advice on her financial portfolio."

"What's she like?"

"Kind of a cold piece of sushi."

Caroline shot me a disapproving look.

"What? You're always harping at me to try different foods. I'm starting with food metaphors."

"Is this *cold piece of sushi* a romantic interest for your padre?" Caroline asked, batting her large green eyes. "The Bella to his Edward?"

I grunted, and my shot met net. "No way!" I said, trotting forward to pick up the ball. "Alice is, like, twenty-nine or something. My dad is . . . I'm not sure. A vampire. And a workahol—a-famer."

Close one. Unrespectable cover-up.

I resumed the rally and blabbered on: "Alice's husband died in a plane crash about a year ago. No joke. I think she's just helping us stay fed as a favor to Aunt Lindsay, keeping herself occupied in the process."

I caught the ball in my left hand, and we stared at each other.

"Why am I so defensive about this?" I asked.

"I don't know," she said.

"That settles it. You have to come over and help spot any old-people sexual tension."

"Okay," she agreed, "if I can make the salad."

"I'm afraid I'm not following. . . ."

"It's green, good for you, and you have to try it."

"Will you be tossing it, or are you going to allow me?"

"I can't believe my boyfriend is such a perv," she said, hitting the ball toward my hurty spot.

Yes, Caroline had turned out to be an otherworldly slice of awesomeness who, unlike Cameo, had her head on straight. In other words, she was an oxymoron. And this moron craved normalcy more than anything. I wanted Caroline, especially because Cameo had started dating Mike Hibbard's friend Andy "No Relation to Mandy" Moore. Even from afar, the scattered glory of Cameo Appearance Parnell continued to confound me. But she was someone else's Scattergory now.

TRACK 23

This Year's Love Lasted Until He Showed Up

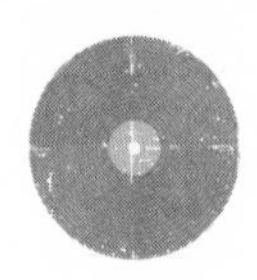

Caroline and I were in the midst of a thigh-curdling figure-eight torture drill when I heard some sort of weird moaning coming from behind me: "Uuuuuuh! Uuuuuuh!" The Jenna Jamesonian sound effect soon accompanied each of my shots, as if I were the source of emission. Ironic, since Alba MacBook and I had paid a nocturnal visit to classic Jenna a few days ago, steering the mouse arrow clear of any clips featuring the modern-day Skeletor version trying to derail my He-Manliness, Master(bator) of the Universe.

"Uuuuuuh!"

Jenna sounded suspiciously like Peter Brady in need of puberty and was getting closer.

Fifty-eight—"Aaaaaah!" Fifty-nine—"Uuuuuuh!"

I saw the porky chop out of the corner of my eye, walking toward my side of the fence, then pressing his other-white-meat face against it: Mike Hibbard. Distracted, I let the ball skid past me as I turned to see how much I owed for this displeasure. It wasn't just him standing there. Andy and Cameo were his two side dishes, and I was positive I hadn't ordered *this* combo platter.

"Hey, Gay!" Mike said.

"Hey, Herp!" I responded automatically.

"I'm *glad* to see you finally found a sport as gay as you are," he said. "G-L-A-A-D."

"Shut up, Mike," Cameo said, looking like she'd rather be anywhere else. "Do you want a ride home or not? My mom is waiting in the parking lot, and she has about twenty minutes of consciousness left."

"I'll just be a minute, Cam," Mike said. "And I'm sorry. That was insensitive. I forgot he was your gay husband for so long."

I shot Cameo a WTF look as Caroline hopped over the net to join me. I felt the moment intensify. These douche-mongrels and Cam-e-ho were bringing the disturbia to my C-line utopia, and it was pissing me off.

"What's going on?" Caroline asked, looking to me, then our visiting trio.

"Nothing," I seethed. "The Herp decided to stop by before he goes to town on the curly fry bin at Arby's. For some reason, he brought two of his outbreaks with him."

I looked at Andy. "Nice of you to let your buddy watch you try to get 'er done while he eats his roast beef. That's what I call some unathletic support."

"Fag," Andy said.

"That's it?" I said. "That played-out word is all you've got? Wow, Cam, you've really outdone yourself."

"Thanks," Cameo said, shooting daggers at both Andy and me. "I needed a date for the Homecoming Dance. *Let's go*, guys."

"Yes," I said, pointing toward the parking lot. "Go join the Herp on his quest to save the McRib."

But Mike couldn't leave on that pithy note. His cheeks blazed red, indicating he wanted more from this visit. Belatedly, I realized I was trapped, that this time the last word wouldn't necessarily be mine.

"It's great that you can practice with your daddy *and* your boyfriend now, Caroline. How is he? He looks kind of like a lesbian to me—"

Caroline, still holding her racket, took a ball from the pocket of her shorts and slammed it into the fence where Mike was standing, causing him to jump back in surprise.

"Sorry, who's the girl again?" she asked.

I snickered, then tensed as Mike made a beeline toward the fence's door.

"Let's finish this, Gay," he said. "I'm sick of your little bitches doing the fighting for you."

As I prepared my unloaded guns for battle, a thunderous bazooka rang out.

"Whoa, whoa, whoa, what is going on here, my little pumpkin squares?"

A riled-up Ms. Lambert hovered to a spot near Cameo and Andy, frizzy gray hair flying in the wind. The woman was both omniscient and omnipresent. How was that possible? No worries, I had the upper hand now. I'd continued grading papers for her during fifth period (my lunch). I enjoyed it, and avoided Cameo and Mike to boot. (Caroline's dad had her utilizing the new weight room and eating protein bars.)

Oddly enough, Ms. Lambert was looking expectantly in my direction. All innocence, all the time, I pointed to Mike. She rolled her eyes and turned to him, hand on her hip. "What's going on, Mike?"

"Nothing," Mike said stupidly, his hand dropping from the door's latch.

"Ha!" she cried. "Really? Because I have a bird's-eye view of these courts from my classroom, and I highly doubt you were opening that door to play mixed doubles with Jay and Caroline."

Mike looked appalled by the notion, and he wasn't the only one.

"And, Jay," she said, pivoting back to me, "please spare me the mixed-doubles puns going through your head right now. And erase that innocent look off your face while you're at it. Mike may have walked over here to start something, but I'm pretty sure you weren't reciting biblical proverbs to keep him at bay."

"Believe me, Ms. Lambert, I want nothing to do with that proverbial Goliath."

I recognized the trace of laughter dancing through her eyes, so I continued. "You said it yourself, Ms. Lambert. We're at the tennis courts, not sucking it on the football field."

"I bet you'd like to be," Mike muttered.

"Your mom—"

"Ahem!" Ms. Lambert growled. "Since the Homecoming Game is next Friday, let me put this in football terms. Aside from my class, the both of you better stay one hundred yards away from each other at all times until I figure out what to do with you."

"I don't think you understand—" I began again.

"All I need to know is that neither of you are mature enough to put the debate behind you. And thank you both once more for the events of that hallowed day, by the way, because your actions will haunt us all for eternity. I walked over to the school's garage today to find out your acting class president, Rene Rotrovich, has made the freshman class Homecoming float look like Katy Perry vomited all over it."

Cameo made a face at Ms. Lambert's comment, no doubt having had something to do with the "We Scored Again and We Liked It" Perry-themed float herself. Almost made me want to laugh, and not just because "Scored" should have been replaced by "Fumbled." Simply put, Cameo had a way of making things hers. When she'd organized a four-square league in sixth grade, it became the most popular sport at recess for a few months. "If you chalk the squares, they will come, bitch," she said to me. And they had, in droves.

Ms. Lambert noticed Cam's indignant reaction: "Ms. Parnell, you have a ride home, correct? Someone other than your friend *Eliza*—"

"Yes," Cameo said quickly. "Andy and I have a ride home. Mike no longer does."

"Oh, no, you don't," Ms. Lambert said, shaking her head. "You'll be taking him, too. I'm not waiting around here to ensure that Beavis and Butt-Head separate amicably. I have important things to do. *American Idol: Rewind* is on tonight. Guarini versus Clarkson."

Ms. Lambert ushered our three visitors to the parking lot, leaving Caroline and me to stare at each other, temporarily on pause.

TRACK 24

Cry Me a River to Sell Her Down

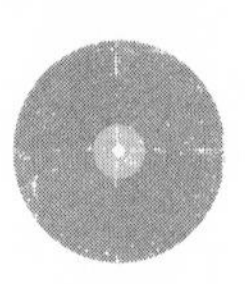

"I can't believe she would do that," I said to Caroline as we resumed with our mini tennis.

"Who?" Caroline asked, striking the ball cleanly. "Ms. Lambert?"

"Huh? No, she was definitely in character. Cameo. I can't believe she would come over here."

"She didn't look like she had much of a choice."

"She could have left Brooks and Dunn behind," I said, sending the ball wide.

"Racket back sooner, Grasshopper," she said, exaggerating her own swing accordingly.

She restarted the rally, saying, "Andy is her boyfriend. Mike is his friend. She probably didn't think you guys would take it that far."

"She knew how far it could go," I insisted, promptly shanking the next ball into the net post.

"How can you be so sure?"

"She knows my history with Mike Bigot better than anyone," I said. "Don't cry for her too much, Argentina. The truth is, she kinda sucks. Be on my side, baby."

Caroline took me literally and hopped over the net, walking toward me. "Maybe you're right. I really can't believe she's dating Andy now, especially since he's friends with Mike Bigot. That's so weird on her part."

She put her arms around my waist and kissed me, my supportive girlfriend.

"You know what concerns me more?" she asked, pulling away and looking directly into my eyes.

"What's that?"

"This whole time you've been talking about Cameo, not even mentioning Mike."

"I like you, not Cameo."

She shook her head, continuing: "I realize that. But you and she are going to have to talk it out eventually. There's too much history. I told you, as lame as it sounds, I don't want to be the naïve girl playing monkey-in-the-middle."

"So you're saying you're not interested in any monkey business?" I asked.

"You're a barrel of laughs, Jay. I'm serious."

"I know. I'm sorry. Will you still come over for dinner?"

"If my dad agrees to it."

"Suck, I forgot about that part."

C-line and I were playing out points when her dad walked up to the court a half hour later. Mr. Richardson was a tall, trim fifty-something with a gray buzz cut. That day, and every day, he rocked a white polo, camouflage cargo shorts, white tube socks, and spotless Stan Smith tennis shoes. He kept an army knife latched to his belt at all times. Quite the statement.

"Hello, sir," I called out in between ground strokes.

I sprinted desperately toward the other side of the court, in pursuit of another one of C-line's deftly angled missiles. And missed the ball.

"Your backhand still looks like you're losing a battle with muscular dystrophy, son."

"Sorry," I said.

Even though he'd served his country in Desert Storm, Mr. Richardson had a penchant for the politically incorrect non sequitur.

He scratched his chin pensively and added, "I'm still not sure you're good enough to drill my daughter properly."

But he had no use for euphemisms. *Little do you know, sir, I have every intention of doing just that. . . .*

"I'm trying, sir," I said.

"Try harder."

"Okay."

Impulsively, I walked over to him. "I was wondering if Caroline could come over for dinner tonight. We're having spaghetti, so she'd be consuming plenty of carbohydrates."

"I'm well aware of how many carbs are in spaghetti," he said curtly.

But he appeared to be thinking over my request, or seeing how he could use it to his advantage.

"Prove it to me," he said.

"Uuuuhh, fifty grams—"

"No, prove to me that you're going to *try harder.* Figure-eight drill, fifty balls in a row. Then Caroline's schedule might free up."

Caroline overheard this condition from her spot near the net.

"Daaaaad!"

"It's okay, Caroline," I called out, bending down to tie my shoe and looking up at Mr. Richardson. "I'm more than happy to be a human ball machine for your daughter, sir."

"Then make it one hundred," he said.

Maybe my double entendres weren't lost on him.

Forty-five minutes later, Caroline and I finally made it to one hundred without me messing up. For the duration of the car ride to my house, she and her dad argued over which tennis player would become the Greatest of All Time, Roger Federer or Rafael Nadal. The convo was a snoozer, but the way they interacted was fascinating.

Mr. Richardson went with the more popular, traditional choice in Federer, no doubt because he was the more aesthetically pleasing player. Caroline stuck to her guns—just as she did on the court—in defense of Nadal.

"How can you vouch for Federer as the GOAT when he can't even beat his greatest rival, Dad?"

"Nadal is a glorified clay-court pusher!" Mr. Richardson retaliated loudly. "Fed has won more Grand Slams, and he's got the French now. Plus, the GOAT needs to have more technical than physical substance. Milk to go with the teat!"

Had to give him points for using "teat" in a sentence. There weren't many of us out there.

"Oh, please," Caroline said. "Are you trapped in a 2005 time capsule? Nadal has a career Grand Slam, too, and he made Federer cry publicly in the process."

He turned to her and smiled. "You had to play the crying card, didn't you?"

"No mercy," she said, smiling in his direction. "I am my father's daughter. Besides, this entire discussion is moot. In my mind, male or female, Monica Seles is the true GOAT. Wah-eee!"

"She got stabbed in the back and started eating everything in sight!" her dad bellowed. "My money is on Steffi Graf."

"Wasn't she accused of tax evasion?" Caroline asked impishly.

And so they began again, eventually making their way to the Chris Evert, Martina Navratilova rivalry.

"Chris was an impenetrable backboard," said Caroline.

"Martina could volley circles around that backboard and then plow it down in her Subaru!" cried Mr. Richardson.

"What about Mary Joe Fernandez?" I said when we pulled into my driveway. "She didn't win any slams or anything, but she's pretty hot."

They both started laughing. "I'm surprised he didn't say Anna Kournikova," Mr. Richardson said to Caroline.

No kidding. How could I have forgotten about the greatest computer virus of all time?

TRACK 25

Dad Likes Her Butt and He Cannot Lie

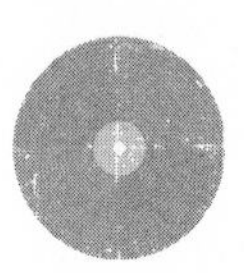

When Caroline and I walked through the door of my house, Dad and his special friend, Alice, were seated at the kitchen bar, already enjoying a bottle of red wine. Given that Dad *and* Mom were nothing but Bud Light connoisseurs, I found the sight of him clutching the skinny stem of his goblet to be quite—how did you say it?—retarded. I heard bubbling sounds coming from the stove, and the air smelled suspiciously of a spaghetti takeover.

"Hey, you two," Dad said warmly.

"Hey, Dad," I said.

"Nice to have you on our turf for a change, Caroline. I hear you've been giving my boy a pretty tough workout on the court."

Dad was beaming with pride. His son had rediscovered sports; he didn't care if my choice had been tennis instead of basketball or baseball. In fact, his endless enthusiasm regarding my practices with Caroline and her dad made it pretty clear I'd been assigning him athletic expectations he never had. Sounded just like something I would do.

"Thanks for having me, Mr. Baker."

"Please, call me Jim."

"My dad would disown me," she demurred.

"He'll never have to know," Dad said, winking at her in his cool-not-creepy way.

"Unless he's outside bugging the place," I said, winking at Dad in my sarcastic way.

"Buffy will get him," he said, but she was sleeping on her dog pillow, deaf to the world.

Dad introduced Caroline to Alice and the two *young* women shook hands daintily. Alice was dressed like a member of the J. Crew rowing team, but she looked nothing like a beastly rower. She was attractive, with her wide smile, perfectly proportioned Cover Girl eyes and nose, and carefully highlighted coiffure. She almost appeared younger than twenty-nine—if not for the telling perma-crease between her eyebrows, a sculpted pair of caterpillars she knitted when she thought no one else was paying attention.

"I hope you don't mind, Jay," Alice said, as if reading from a teleprompter. "I saw the ingredients lying out and started dinner. I figured you guys would be hungry when you returned."

"That's cool," I said. "But I can take over from here if you want."

Alice smiled at me. It was clear she found my offer to be . . . unappetizing.

"No, that's okay," she said smoothly. "I have a new sauce I've been pretty excited to try. I hope you guys like it."

New sauce. I fully anticipated not liking, or wanting, Alice's new sauce—both literally and metaphorically. I wanted plain old Ragú meat sauce like we always had in this house. What I didn't so much desire was anyone getting Prego with ideas on how to change things.

Dad and Alice both took a drink of wine, glancing meaningfully at each other.

I looked at Caroline, and before my flared nostrils could reach their maximum wingspan, she whispered into my ear, "Just try the sauce, Jay. It might not be that bad."

"It smells like Buffy's Alpo, and I hate it already," I whispered back.

Ten awkward minutes later, Alice and Caroline started setting the dining room table, which Dad and I had pledged to never, ever sit at because the angle made watching TV difficult.

"Spaghetti is so easy," Alice said, placing linen napkins on the plates instead of our usual paper towels. "And it will be nice to eat dinner at a table, for once. I don't know how long it's been since . . ."

She trailed off, and my dormant sympathy nerve spazzed to life as I remembered her lost husband. Understandable that she would want to enjoy a dinner with a few companions, considering she was the widow of a *plane crash victim*.

"This all looks really tasty, Alice," I said amenably. "I'm impressed you coerced my dining-room-averse father into agreeing to a sit-down dinner."

"I have my ways," she said, smiling at my father.

Sympathy going, going, gone: flagrant flirting foul ball called on Alice. Why were she and Dad suddenly so open about their fondness for each other?

"Caroline," I said, walking over to Sleeping Buffy and leaning down to pet her head.

"Yep?"

She was helping Alice bring over our drinks: two more pretentious glasses of wine for the happy couple, a sophisticated can of Mountain Dew for me, and a seltzer on the rocks minus the alka for C-line.

"Let's take Buffy outside. She looks like she needs to shit."

"Language, Jay," Dad said. He sat down at the table without difficulty, even though Alice was busy removing his balls.

I nudged the dog with my foot. "Sorry," I said, but I was talking to Buffy.

Caroline and my somnambulant canine dutifully followed me outside.

"What the hell?" I said to Caroline, stretching my arms to denote the exact size of my hell. "Forget *Twilight*, why do I feel like we stumbled into a bad Danielle Steel novel? Will the plane crash widow and potential divorcé learn to love again?"

"They're probably starting to feel more comfortable being that way toward each other around you."

"Why in the world would they feel a crazy thing like that?"

"Because tonight you're with me," Caroline reasoned. "It's a foursome, essentially—a situation where men and women naturally pair off into couples. They're less inclined to hide their feelings as a result."

"I'm more inclined to throw up my chicken patty as a result of their feelings."

"I told you to stop eating those at lunch," she said. "Just try to relax. I'm right here."

For the first time that day, I lost sight of my issues and really *looked* at Caroline, acknowledging the underlying sadness in her eyes. All this talk about me. . . . What was *she* stressing over? Cameo? Her mother?

"Are you okay?" I asked, grabbing her hands and bringing her close to me.

"Yep," she said unconvincingly.

"Tell me what's going on."

"I'm fine," she said, gently pulling away and kissing me on the cheek. "Just hungry. Let's eat."

I decided not to press the issue and called for Buffy, who just then had settled on a spot. She was very picky, and I'd disturbed her pooping peace. She gave me a disdainful look and went searching for another patch of grass. We waited a few more minutes for her to finish her business by Dad's Ohio State Buckeyes flag before going back inside.

"So, how long have you been playing tennis, Caroline?" Alice asked, our foursome now seated at the dinner table.

"Ever since I could walk," Caroline responded. "My dad gave me a tennis ball in lieu of a pacifier."

Alice laughed—a short, to-the-point sound that was nothing like the prolonged cackle of my mother.

"I wish I was joking," Caroline said, smiling. "But he means well."

Yeah, but did anyone else think this spaghetti was disgusting? I took a drink.

"What do you do?" Caroline asked Alice shyly. "I mean, as a career?"

"I'm a hair stylist," Alice said, "but I haven't been working much lately. Just here and there when someone I know needs a trim."

According to the Indian Lake rumor mill, Alice had been wrapped up in a wrongful death suit with the airline responsible for the plane crash; until recently, when she'd accepted a settlement worth millions. She was one loaded twenty-nine-year-old, so what exactly did she want with my family-man father?

"My nose hairs could use a trim," Dad said.

"Here we go," I said, setting my fork on my plate.

"I'm thinking of taking off an inch or two," he added. "How much will that run me, Alice?"

He was being playful—the attentive "kissy-kissy!" Dad whom Mom had lost somewhere along the way.

Alice looked at him reproachfully, yet flirtatiously. "You're on your own with that one, Jim."

I felt Caroline's hand brush mine underneath the table. At first I thought it might have been an accident, but then she grabbed my pinky finger with hers. Instantly, I felt better. C-line was pinky-promising me that I wasn't alone in dealing with this—yet another new development in my parents' relationship saga, cast of characters still growing.

Crazy Daddy Richardson was early, of course. He honked

the horn three times before C-line could put her plate in the dishwasher.

"I can get that, Caroline," Alice offered.

"No, it's okay," Caroline insisted. "He can wait."

Dad and I stood back and observed until they were finished, then I escorted Caroline to the door.

"Sorry I was such a basket case tonight," I said. "And today, too."

"It's okay, Jay."

"Can I make it up to you? Can we play tennis tomorrow and hang out afterward? No distractions."

"Sure. If my dad lets me."

"He will," I assured her. "He's in my corner now. I have to go to Mom's, but you can come over there. After dinner, she usually kills some Nicorette and takes a booty call from Keith in her bedroom. She'll leave us alone."

"Cool," she said, shifting her weight.

"Are you sure you're okay?"

"We'll talk tomorrow at your mom's."

"Cameo?" I probed.

"Nope. Promise. Kiss, please."

I looked over to the bar and confirmed that Dad and Alice were still yukking it up in their own little world. I leaned forward and kissed Caroline just as Mr. Richardson let forth a particularly lengthy *beeeeeep*. Sperm donor to the most beautiful creature on the planet or not, I cursed him for salting my game nearly as much as Alice had her sauce. I was going to kiss his daughter for three more seconds, if it was the last thing I did before he killed me.

TRACK 26

STRANGE HOW HARD IT RAINS WHEN IT POURS

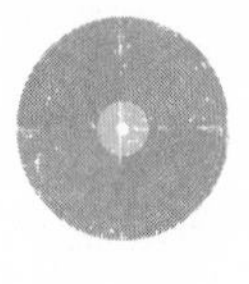

Alice and Dad had moved to the living room, still chatting; I was seated at the kitchen bar doing my human biology homework—Sleeping Buffy's head perched atop my left foot like a concrete gargoyle—when my sister pulled into the garage a half hour later. Things were about to get interesting.

Abby walked in without a word to anyone and sat down at the bar beside me, texting frantically.

Dad and Alice said hello, Abby grunted, and they continued jumping down each other's esophaguses with really boring stories about their respective childhoods. Alice mentioned something about the farm she grew up on having a chicken coop. I flipped to the index of my book, looking for the plural form of "esophagus." Esophagi. Good to know.

Unexpectedly, Alice vacated her seat and walked into the kitchen. She took a foil-wrapped plate from the oven and placed it on the bar in front of Abby. I saw that she'd labeled the foil "Abby" with a Sharpie, and I stopped myself from saying it was never in danger of being eaten by someone else. Instead, I watched the two ladies attentively.

"We saved you some grub, Abby," Alice said.

For no good reason, I noted Alice's use of the word "we"; she was wary of taking too much credit for providing Abby her meal. Smart. She didn't want my sister to feel as though she owed her something. I also noticed her mistaking "grub" for passable slang, but I found this endearing. I expected Abby to deliver a prickly thanks—possibly while texting—and leave it at that.

Instead, she smiled and said, "Thank you, Alice. How've you been?"

Huh? As Abby picked up her fork and started eating, I examined her neck to see if Dad had implanted some kind of microchip there. Abby's appetite and goodwill toward hen were two surprises this turkey didn't trust.

Looking pleased by the response, Alice said, "I'm doing well, thanks. Trying to keep myself busy."

"That's cool," Abby said.

"Yeah . . . ," Alice said, trailing off again.

"This is good," Abby lied, gesturing toward the spaghetti.

"Thanks," Alice said.

That was it. Their conversation had run the gamut, but I was inclined to declare it a raging success, anyway. Dad walked over and started rubbing Abby's shoulders, and she softened even more.

"How's my Homecoming Queen?" he asked.

"I'm okay, Daddy," she said, putting down her fork. "I found a dress online today."

Sweet, Abby was taking the bait I'd left for her earlier that morning. While she was still asleep, I'd crawled out of my floor bed and logged into her computer, typing in the BCBG URL Mom had texted me the night before: "She'll love this dress, Jay."

"Excellent," Dad said. "How much?"

"I need your credit card."

"Uh-oh," he said.

Abby's phone buzzed. She answered it, kissed Dad on the cheek, and headed for her room—already scolding Eric for being Eric.

"Jay!" Alice said, apparently remembering something. "Have you heard of Maple Lane Tennis Club?"

"Yep, I used to take lessons there."

"I wanted to tell you this while Caroline was here . . . darn. Anyway, I was bored today and called to ask about their junior programs. Your dad said Caroline can't always play with you. I thought you might want to practice against some different opponents."

"That would be awesome," I said. "But Dad and Mom work late a lot, and I'm vehicularly challenged."

"Well, I was thinking I could take you," Alice said, looking somewhat embarrassed. "If it's okay with your dad and mom, that is."

"Oh," I said.

"I'm all right with it," Dad jumped in.

The offer had caught me entirely off guard. Was Alice trying to compete with Mom? I couldn't help but speculate.

"I don't have much on my plate these days," Alice added.

"Alice, let's have a quick smoke," Dad said, impatiently tapping her on the shoulder.

"I'm trying to have a conversation," Alice said, eyeing him playfully.

"C'mon," he said. "Run like this."

He lifted his legs high in the air and ran toward the garage door. I figured Alice would follow primly, for fear of looking unladylike, but she surprised me again by lifting up her coltish legs and galloping after him.

"Okay, but then I have to go home," she said to him before calling back over her shoulder to me. "Let me know about tennis, Jay."

"Sure," I said. "Thanks."

Just when the playlist of my life seemed to be in order, this day had come along and jammed the shuffle button. The scene with Mike and Cameo, my reaction to it, Caroline being weird, Alice making her move on Dad, Abby's seemingly medicated reaction to that . . . I was more discombobulated than ever.

When Dad walked back in from the garage, he took one look at my face and sensed my ambivalence. He whistled for Buffy and me, pointing back behind him in the direction of the garage. I looked down at the dog. She heard him, for once, but her eyes blinked reluctantly.

"Buffy and I don't feel like smoking, Dad."

"C'mon," he said, whistling again. "Smoking is a great idea, buddy, but that's not what I have in mind."

Obediently, we followed him outside. Dad headed toward the bin that contained our dusty sporting equipment and grabbed the basketball on top, palming it effortlessly with his right hand and smiling at me.

"You may be a big tennis stud now, but I'm curious to see if you're good enough to beat your Big Dad at P-I-G. After all, I am an Olympic gold medalist in basketball."

Dad was an alleged Olympic gold medalist in many sports, although all his medals had vanished mysteriously. "They made us give 'em back in those days," he claimed. Only his high school scrapbook remained—the lacy, Grandma-made yawnthology he'd been threatening to show my sister and me ever since we were old enough to run away screaming for Mom.

Dang, that was a good family memory—so piercing it made my eyes water a bit. I leaned down to pet Buffy and avert Dad's gaze.

"Whaddaya say, bud?" he asked, sounding hopeful. "Shoot a few hoops with me?"

I relented. "Okay, but are you sure Larry Bird would approve of those boat shoes?"

He slaughtered me the first game, and then the next, sinking nearly every shot. I finally started hitting something other than air in the third, yet still found myself down a "P" to Dad's litter- and letter-free pen.

"Caroline seems like a great girl," he said, banking in a bunny shot.

"Yeah, she's awesome," I said, missing it for a P-I. "Not sure what she's doing with me."

"We Baker men have our own brand of charm," Dad said.

His tongue jutted out between his lips in concentration as he drilled another shot from the foul line. He blew out the invisible flame on his hand and looked at me expectantly.

"What's your take on Alice?" he asked.

"She's nice," I said noncommittally, stepping up to the hash mark he'd painted several years ago. "Generous of her to offer me a ride to tennis."

"Yes," Dad said. "From what I know of her, she's pretty selfless. And extremely independent."

Unlike Mom? I bricked the ball into the backside of the rim, but Christmas came early and Baby Jesus carried it forward and through the net.

"Snizzle," I said, drawing the "s" out.

"Beautiful shot."

"Thanks."

"So what do you *really* think of Alice?" he asked, pausing a moment to dribble between his boat shoes.

"I dunno, Dad," I said impatiently. "What do *you* think of her?"

"I like her," he said, attempting a Magic Johnson hook shot I had no hope of duplicating.

He barely missed, and I grabbed the ball and dribbled over to the side of the court, about fifteen feet from the basket: Mom's favorite shot.

I made it. Score one for Team Mom.

"Booyah, Big D."

Dad rebounded the ball, dribbled it over, and made the shot.

"Alice . . . she's nothing like our family, Dad."

"For sure," Dad said. "But if I teach you one thing about people, Jay, aside from the fact that most of them don't have enough insurance, let it be this: we're all a product of our environment. You, me, Alice—everyone. Alice grew up in a farmer's household where things weren't exactly warm and fuzzy. She's not the best communicator, but her heart's in the right place."

I missed my next shot (a layup), and he made his (a three-pointer).

"Based on that anti-Darwin philosophy, are you and Mom in the process of screwing me up for life?" I asked.

I launched the ball up into the air from the three-point line. It curled around the basket and bounced out. P-I-maybe G. Dad needed to prove it for the win.

"I'd like to think we've done a pretty decent job so far," he said, grabbing the ball.

"You have, but—"

"We'll figure things out, your mom and I," Dad promised.

"The sooner the better."

"I agree," he said, dribbling. "I know I work too much, but I want to make sure my family is taken care of in the long term. My parents—your grandparents—didn't plan for retirement, and now they're stuck hoping Social Security doesn't run out. That scares me, and your mom doesn't get that."

I sat down on the concrete with my arms around my knees.

"But do you still love her, Dad?" I asked as he was setting up to seal my fate.

He stopped his shot and looked over at me. “I’ll be honest with you, Jay. Things still aren’t looking too promising for your mom and me. But Keith or no Keith, marriage or no marriage, I’ll always love her.”

Then drop the ball (on Alice) and prove *that*, Dad.

He dribbled a few more times; I closed my eyes and heard the sound of the ball swishing through the net.

TRACK 27

Dick and Some Jocks

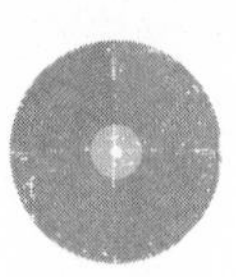

Abby drove me to school the next morning, the first five minutes of the ride observed in silent deference to her baby-eating mood. I had plenty to say, but I waited patiently for her cue. She would talk when she was good 'n' ready, or she might never speak again. It could go either way.

Distracting chatter was hazardous to my health, anyway. A veritable Ms. Daisy in need of a driver, I wasn't sure how Abby was licensed by the DMV. But I would never tell that to her, even as she pulled into the gas station a good ten feet away from the nozzle and handed me her debit card.

"This is a full-service gas station," she said, nodding toward the pump.

"Of course it is," I said, getting out.

I stretched the rubber tube as far as it would go and switched the automatic pumping lever back. A cappuccino urge surged to my frontal lobe, so I ran into the store while the gas guzzled and purchased two before Abby could yell at me to do otherwise.

Once back in the car, I wafted the steaming cup toward her Lord Voldemort nostrils. She accepted my offering and put the car in gear. Sipping the beverage soon lifted her drooping eyes and her crappy outlook on humanity.

"That spaghetti was disgusting last night," she said.

"Finally!" I cried, drinking too deeply and burning my epiglottis off. "Holy schnikes, where have you been? Why were you so nice to her?"

Abby shrugged her familiar shrug of cool indifference. The shrug that had broken a thousand high school hearts—and my mother's.

"I'm over it. Sick of worrying about our parents. They're moving on, so why shouldn't we?"

"I'm struggling."

"Obviously," she said.

"Dad's Alice dalliance means he's just as guilty of moving on as Mom."

"Your mother," Abby said pointedly, "chose to embark on her little skankfest before her marriage was over. Not the same thing."

"Still," I persisted, "Dad's moving pretty fast, wouldn't you say? Aunt Lindsay introduces them two weeks ago, now they're splitting a bottle of merlot and getting crunk over Alice's corn-shucking narrative? And I'm not being rude—yes, I am—but she's kind of a Scientology experiment gone wrong. She's a Katie Holmes. Only ten years older than you, and dresses nice enough, but she's an ol'-fashioned butter churner."

"Your paranoia is getting to you, Jay."

"Maybe," I admitted. "She did offer to drive me to tennis lessons."

"Who does that?" Abby said. "Take her up on the offer, loser. Who cares if she's a Katie?"

Abby pulled into a huge parking space, still managing to skew her car crooked. Before we got out, I needed to take advantage of her newfound laissez-faire, Lazzie-bear attitude. I'd summoned her over to Mom's for their first Maury! Maury! go-around; the least I could do was schedule the reunion.

"If you're so *over* everything, then you should come to Mom's for dinner tonight."

"Can't," she said. "The *Examiner* is taking the Homecoming Court's picture."

"Tomorrow night, then," I said.

"Eric's sister has a seventh-grade volleyball game."

"You're kidding me with that one, right?"

"He wants me to go."

"Since when do you do what Eric wants?"

"True."

"Just stay for an hour and pretend to eat," I said. "Do it for me, if nothing else. I'm sick of fielding questions about you. I only have so many pregnancy jokes."

"Fine."

Caroline was waiting for me by my locker, looking sexy. She wore a comfortable-looking hooded sweatshirt and tight jeans, her wavy hair down for a change and hanging past her shoulders. Her skin was tanned from our tennis sessions, and her face bore no makeup except for the sheen of Burt's Bees on her lips.

"Hey, you," she said.

"Hey," I said, kissing her.

She broke the kiss, so I began fiddling with my locker combo.

"How are—"

"How did things end up with your dad last night?" she asked, interrupting me.

What was her deal? I wondered again why the girl who'd been so open before she really knew me (e.g., the tell-all drinking game we'd played after detention) suddenly seemed so reluctant to tell me anything.

"All is well," I said. "And I really mean that. Dad and I talked, and believe it or not my intense sister just helped me realize that I should let the Skittles fall where they may."

"Acceptance is the first step, Grasshopper!" she said, smiling widely and squeezing my arm. "You're reminding me of a man right now."

"Every once in a while I'll stumble upon some testosterone," I said, spinning the wheel for the final time and opening my locker.

A colorful piece of paper drifted to the floor by my feet. Not recognizing it, I bent down to pick it up and immediately wished I hadn't. No joke, it was a printout of a big, giant, purple, vein-filled, disgusting penis. Near the hairy sack were the words "Thought you might like to bend over and take this later, fag."

Mike Hibbard. That swine-flu-spreading STD. Leave it to the Herp to resort to unoriginal locker retaliation. Really, he couldn't even spring for spray paint? His penile sneak-attack was far more effective with my girlfriend standing over me, though, staring down at her boyfriend holding some dude's fatty between his fingertips.

I balled up the page and looked around to see if anyone had noticed besides Caroline. Indeed, there they were: Mike, Andy, and a few other guys, chuckling amongst themselves about ten feet away. And behind them, there *she* was: Cameo Appearance, looking as beautifully listless as ever.

Caroline lifted me up by my arm, grabbing the crumpled penis from my hand.

"C'mon, Jay," she said firmly. "I'm not letting you get into it with him today."

She walked me to first period and massaged my shoulders for a minute before the bell rang. They were up to my ears with tension. It was *on*.

TRACK 28

Ms. Lambert Told Me, There'll Be Days Like This

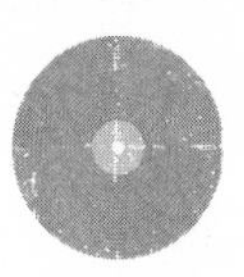

By Ms. Lambert's fourth-period government class, I was a time bomb. At the board when I walked in, teacher made sure to shoot her pet a disapproving look—presumably for yesterday's tit-for-tat with Mike—before I sat down at my desk in the front row. I saw Mike out of the corner of my eye, sitting to my right toward the back of the classroom. The dude definitely had some tits, and he was looking more self-satisfied than any pregnant male teenager had a right to be.

The bell rang. Ms. Lambert launched into a real lemon of a lecture on important Supreme Court decisions, but it gave me the opportunity to make lemonade in my head and plot my revenge. Considering I sat in the front row, I should have known better than to let my eyes leave the board.

"I'm sorry, Mr. Baker," Ms. Lambert said, interrupting my reverie. "Is *Roe v. Wade* not an important enough decision for you to grace me with your attention?"

Somebody cried out "Mama!" in a baby voice, and I had a pretty good idea it was Jennifer trying to cover for me. I'd buy her a Mountain Dew later.

"I already read the chapter," I said.

"Oh! My fault, snookums. Why am I up here, then? If you have all the answers, by all means, take it away."

Inspiration struck.

"Thanks for the Kudos Bar, Ms. Lambert, but I don't know everything yet—"

"Then pay attention!"

"Hold up, I have a question."

She sighed. "Yes?"

"Does *Roe v. Wade* apply to guys?"

There were a few snickers from the peanut gallery.

"Please, Jay," she said, rolling her eyes. "You've wasted too much of my life this week as it is."

"No," I said. "I'm serious. I know someone, a guy in our school, who might be fifteen and pregnant. I just want to be sure he's aware of his options. He's really sensitive."

I nodded my head in Mike's direction, and Jennifer and a few others started laughing. I could tell Ms. Lambert was suppressing a smile, but she couldn't let on that she found this amusing. I felt Mike's eyes lasering a hole in my skull.

"Your concern is touching, Jay, but why don't you *row* your eyes back up to the board and *wade* on over to my desk after class?"

"I grade papers for you, remember?"

"I think we have a few other items on the docket today."

Everyone oohed with interest, and Ms. Lambert began writing extra homework assignments on the board to shut them up.

Fifth period was also Ms. Lambert's planning period, so we had the classroom to ourselves. Usually, we spent the entire time outdoing each other with witticisms, but today she had more serious matters on her mind. She was at her desk; I was still at mine.

"So are you trying to suspend yourself, Jay, or is your behavior today and yesterday some sort of cry for help? Do we need to have an intervention?"

"I'm clean."

"Then how am I going to punish you?"

"I have an explanation."

"Start talking!"

"Mike put a little surprise in my locker this morning, and I wanted to be sure he knew I appreciated the gesture. I'm sorry for using your class to serve my purpose."

"At least someone got something out of it today."

"It was pretty brutal—"

"Hush," she said. "Only I can make fun of my lectures."

"Back to Mike," I prompted.

"Ah, yes," she said. "So, Mike violated your dual restraining order. Didn't take long, did it? I'll deal with him later. If there's a next time, you need to take the problem straight to me and get over it at home. You're lucky I'm a teacher who pretends to care. Is getting back at Mike really worth jeopardizing your academic record?"

"It is when he raises the stakes in front of Caroline," I said. "She and I are playing enough double jeopardy as it is."

"Girl trouble?" she ventured, her morbid curiosity piqued.

"Inappropriate topic to discuss with a teacher."

"Maybe," she said, "but if I had my nosy druthers about me, I'd say you're caught in one of America's favorite pastimes: the love triangle. You've set yourself up perfectly, in part thanks to my Caroline encouragement. Gawd, I miss *Melrose Place*! The original incarnation, that is."

"You're one evil mastermind who's too good for the CW," I said.

"I prefer fairy godmother," she said, "but I'll take that as a compliment. And Caroline is lovely, isn't she?"

"One of a kind."

"Ha! But I saw the way you were looking at Cameo yesterday. Someone's trying to have his cake and eat it, too."

"I don't like Cameo's cake."

"But you like her icing—"

"Objection," I said. "Uncomfortable, Your Honor."

"Overruled," she said. "Want to know which one I think you should date?"

"No."

"NEITHER!" she screamed.

When students had the gall to ask for a bathroom pass during *her time*, Ms. Lambert gave them a giant foot-long courtroom gavel, stuffed with cotton and designed to make them look ridiculous when they walked down the hallway. She grabbed it from her desk and threw it at me, hitting me in the face.

"You're not ready to date anyone, Jay! Pardon my French, but you need to wake up and find an identity. Not Caroline's. Not Cameo's. Not Eliza Doolittle's. When I encouraged you to get acquainted with Caroline, I didn't think you were going to adopt her sport, too. Do you even like tennis?"

"It's okay," I said, shrugging. "It gets me out of the house."

"That's great, future Unabomber, but what do *you* really like? Maybe then you can figure out *whom* you like."

"I like . . . pizza."

"Get out of my classroom."

"Okay, okay. Let me think about it for a minute. Jeez."

Hers was a valid question. What did I, Jay Baker, truly enjoy doing?

A few minutes later: "I have no idea."

"Let's think about it a different way, then. Do you have any talents, any assets aside from being a pain in my ass?"

"I think I'm pretty funny."

"Mwahahahaha!"

I stared at her.

"Oops, you were being serious for once. Okay, let me write that down so I remember. Jay. Is. Funny. I can work with that. We need to find a positive outlet for you to express your little jokes through."

"I already have a MacBook that I write stuff in almost every night," I said.

"Oh, how precious. Your very own Doogie Howser journal."

"Fine, what's my punishment?"

She laughed. "No, no. I think journals are great for the

person writing them, but relatively boring to everyone else. You've handed in a few papers to me, and I can see you're miles ahead of your 'See Spot Run' classmates in the language department. What about a blog?"

I groaned. "Everybody has a blog."

"So?"

"So, not everybody needs to have a voice."

"I don't care about everybody," Ms. Lambert said. "Yes! That's your assignment. You need to have an interesting, school-appropriate blog up and running by Friday, or I'm bestowing you with two weeks of detention."

"For what?" I asked incredulously.

"You know *for what*. For bringing up male pregnancy in my classroom. For generally stressing me out. Do it. We'll see how funny you really are."

My phone buzzed loudly. I reached into my pocket to hit the side button, but it was too late.

"I heard that!" she said, pointing to the poster on her wall—a picture of Uncle Sam with the tagline, *I want your cell phone*.

"Don't know what you're talking about."

"I rue the day that baby boomers began thinking it necessary to give their teenage sons and daughters iPhones," she said. "Making y'all stupider, one tweet at a time."

"I have to go to the bathroom," I said.

"Bladder balderdash, you just want to read your text."

I waved the stuffed gavel/bathroom pass and walked out before she could say anything. In the bathroom, I flipped open my phone to see Cameo's name on the screen. The body of her text was one for the record books. . . .

> "Jaaaaay. Read that like Stella from *Streetcar.* Don't act like you don't know how. I just broke up with Andy at lunch. I'm sorry for your man-meat porn surprise. I'm sorry for letting them come over to the courts the other day. I'm so sorry for going out with him in the first place. You know how I am. I am . . . a hopelessly bad decision maker. And I miss you something awful. I feel like someone cut off my arm and is beating me over the head with it every time I think about calling you and I can't because things got weird. Can we please talk? What are you doing tonight???"

I was playing tennis with Caroline. Then she and I were going over to Mom's. No room for third wheels, love triangles, or ménage à . . . it's always best to keep one's options open. I decided not to text Cam back. Then my stomach started to rumble. Tail between my legs, I entered a stall and pulled down my pants compliantly. Served me right.

TRACK 29

Too Late to Apologize for Being Shady?

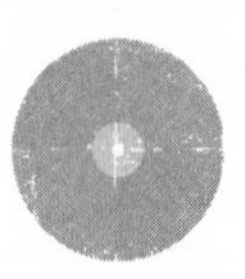

Caroline seemed preoccupied at practice. She was missing shots during some of our points, which meant I was managing to win a few. Her dad—observing us for the last hour—didn't find my default victories to be an acceptable departure from the norm. And even though Mom was waiting in the parking lot to take us both to Holiday Shores, he demanded that Caroline practice exclusively with him for one more hour.

"Go stretch," he said to me. "You look like you just escaped from Shady Pines. I'll bring Caroline by later."

Shady Pines. That rang a bell.

"Sir, are you a fan of *The Golden Girls?*"

"Go."

For maybe the fiftieth time that day, I asked Caroline if she was okay. She nodded and grabbed my pinky, promising she'd be at Mom's ASAP.

Reluctantly, I walked toward Mom's SUV. It was parked

facing the courts, and I could see her through the windshield. Her signature aviator sunglasses covered her eyes, and she appeared to be talking to herself.

I opened the door and stepped up to my seat.

"Where's Caroline?" Mom asked.

"Her dad is making her practice for another hour," I said.

"Aw, poor girl, should I go talk to him?"

"Not unless you're interested in running suicides."

A voice from the back of the SUV: "Ugh, suicides. We had to do those at cheerleading once. Katie Tracey and her cottage-cheese thighs couldn't even finish one. God, is there anything more annoying than a roly-poly girl on the squad who can't do a back handspring?"

Surprised, I looked behind me to see—who else?—Cameo Appearance Parnell, stretched out in the backseat with her head resting on her cheerleading bag.

"I can think of something more annoying," I said.

I belted up and Mom drove away.

"What are you doing here, Cameo?" I asked, unable to mask my irritation.

Surprised by the edge in my tone, Mom's speed dropped from fifty-four MPH to fifty-three.

"Don't be rude, Jay," she admonished.

"No, no," Cameo said. "It's okay, Kim. Jay and I haven't been getting along as famously ever since . . . well, anyway."

Mom and I ran our fingers through our hair, fidgeting through the awkward silence.

Cameo filled it with another hot-air balloon: "I needed a ride home from practice, Jay. Andy *was* my ride, but you know how that turned out. Mom isn't picking up her phone, and Dad is covering for a bartender friend at Eddie's. I'm one HOT potato, and I'm starving."

"I invited Cam to stay for pizza before I take her home," Mom said, turning to me and smiling. "She and Caroline are friends, right?"

Mom's intentions were good. She hadn't known how strained things were between Cameo and me. Therefore, in an effort to ignore the cheerleader and save my sanity, I told Mom about Abby agreeing to dinner tomorrow night. She looked ecstatic. We talked about her Homecoming Queen duties for the rest of the way to Holiday Shores—which was rapidly becoming Ohio's trailer-park answer to Melrose Place.

The TV was on and I was sitting on the recliner; Cameo was on the love seat—site of our ill-fated make-out session—with *my mother.* Not much had been said in the last twenty minutes.

Mom turned to Cameo and asked, "Do you want to look through Jay's scrapbooks with me?"

"Do I?!" Cameo responded.

Mom was punishing me for not playing happy host to our guest. She walked over to the bookshelf and returned with two large collections of gawky childhood development. As if it weren't bad enough Cameo had witnessed the metadorkosis firsthand.

"I want to see Jay as a baby," Cameo said. "Was he born with that same Sour Patch Kid expression that's on his face right now?"

"Good one," I said.

"It talks!" Cameo said.

"Don't worry, sweetie," Mom said to Cameo, visions of butt-naked bathtub pictures dancing in her head. "You're gonna see it all."

Mercifully, Keith rang from the bar a few minutes later, and Mom took the call back in her room to digest his NutraSweet nothings in private.

"I really like what you've done with your rat tail here," Cameo said, flipping through the pages.

"Thanks."

A few more minutes passed and Cameo put away the albums.

"Uhhhh," she said, sitting back down. "Do you want to play Monopoly?"

"Advance token to No Thanks Avenue," I said.

Even though I'd texted Caroline a warning (no response), I wasn't about to be caught alone under the boardwalk with Cameo. Besides, it was time for Cam to accept the news that she'd taken second prize in the Cameo/Caroline beauty contest of my mind.

"I really am sorry to intrude like this, Jay," Cameo said. "Surprised?"

"Nonsense, I completely expected you to be hanging out in my mom's car."

"I know, right? How annoying am I, popping out of the *proverbial* birthday cake like that? Especially when I know how much you loathe disruptions to your schedule."

"I'm starting to get used to them," I muttered. "And you can't use 'proverbially' like that."

"Sure you can," she said. "Anyway, when you didn't respond to my text, I figured this would be the perfect opportunity for us to hash out our shiz."

"Caroline will be here shortly," I reminded her. "Let's bust out the pooper-scooper another time."

"Honestly, Jay, I didn't know she was coming here, too, until your mom showed up at school."

"Gotcha. I know. Doesn't matter now."

"Why are you being such a chach?" she asked, frustrated. "I know things got a little wonky for a while there, but it wasn't all me. And I apologized for my end of it. Where's your apology?"

"It's in the trash can with the penis your ex-boyfriend and his friend gave me."

"I had nothing to do with that, and you know it."

"Of course not," I said. "You just sat back and watched."

"*I said I was sorry, Jay.* Excuse me for wanting my best friend's forgiveness. I gave birth to your sea monkeys, for the love."

Ouch. She knew I loved those sea monkeys.

Cameo took out her phone and dialed her mom. No answer. "She's probably having one of her Marilyn Monroe moments," she surmised.

"Huh?"

"When Mom fancies herself suicidal, she'll take two Mother's Little Helpers and pass out on the bathroom floor."

"That's messed up," I said.

Cameo shrugged, looking sad.

Things hadn't been easy for either of us. I needed to be nicer, more understanding. I walked into the kitchen and grabbed a couple Mountain Dews, handing one to her when I returned.

"I'm sorry for letting our parents get in the way of our friendship," I said, sitting back down and popping the tab. "But things have changed, Cameo. I have a great girl in Caroline, and I don't want her thinking I'm hung up on you."

"Meaning what?" she asked.

"Meaning you and I can't play Barbie and Ken at each other's dream houses anymore."

Worrying Caroline had arrived just in time to hear me say that, I looked toward the opened front door—the cool autumn air blowing in from the *empty* Florida room.

"Just because you and Caroline are playing tennis together and kissing publicly, doesn't mean you have to stop hanging out with me."

"Welcome to my world, Cam. Are you forgetting all those times you dated some wanker and I was left to babysit myself?"

"I still called you."

"Not once did you come over while you were revisiting your low-quality relationship with Wade over the summer."

She wrinkled her snub nose. "You don't make it easy on people, Jay, being that you never leave the house. But whatever, that's not my point. We have too much history—"

"My parents have a long history, too," I muttered. "It all gets thrown out with the baby and the bathwater in the end."

"Oh, cut the cord already, Jay," Cameo snapped. "I'm going through something similar with my parents, and although you assume I don't care, I do. Even you have to admit that a person can play the victim for only so long. Look at Ashley Judd, the damsel in distress in the same movie over and over again. After a while, people stop buying a ticket. Your parents might not be getting back together, Jay. You should try dealing with it."

"What do you think I've been doing?" I said angrily. "That's all I've done is *deal with it*. I didn't choose for your dad and my mom to hump. And I can't wave a magic stick, Lil' Cam, and choose how fast I get over it. Even if you think you can. Why don't you go numb your emotions with another 3D-bag avatar from Mike Hibbard's tribe?"

"I'm starting to forget why I wanted to have this conversation," she said. "Never mind."

She walked out into the Florida room and sat down on one of the plastic chairs. I followed her.

"No point in taking your foot off the pedal now, Cam," I said, sitting down across from her. "You obviously wanted to go there. So go."

"Fine. What you've really been doing is playing a buttload of tennis, a sport you kind of/sort of like, with Caroline to avoid everything instead of dealing with anything. Because you're an avoider. You think I'm disgusting for dating Andy to distract myself from my crappy home life? News flash, you're a hypocrite."

Even though Cameo had a point—similar to the one Ms. Lambert had made—I was too stubborn to admit it.

"Don't compare Apples to Douchebags," I said. "My relationship with Caroline is different. I really like her. A lot. You and Andy lasted, what, two weeks before you gave him your notice?"

Cameo took a deep breath and leaned forward. Her blue eyes were murky with emotion when she spoke next.

"I know you may find this hard to believe, Jay, but I've liked you for a long, long time. I was never in a big rush, because I always thought we'd end up together. When you and Caroline started spending so much time together, I panicked and grabbed the first person available. I know. I'm sweet. But there she blows."

"Naaaaaw" was all I could manage to say, really, really uncomfortable now. This wasn't the way this was supposed to go down. Cameo had always been, well, Cameo Appearance Parnell. I'd never expected her to reciprocate my feelings.

"It's true," she said. "You've been the one I've wanted since our days ruling the four-square court. It's so obvious if you think about it. The way I flirt with you—"

"You flirt with the cafeteria ladies to get extra fries," I said.

"They like it," she retorted. "And you weren't complaining when you were the one eating them."

"This just doesn't make any sense," I said. "I'm the one who liked *you* forever."

"You say you liked me, Jay," Cameo said patiently. "But aside from that day we kissed, did you ever show me? No. And didn't I respond in your favor? You're not stupid. You just play dumb to *avoid* dealing with your discomfiture. You could tell how much I wanted you in that moment. Until I figured out that my duty-free dad had ruined everything.... This is starting to get embarrassing," she said. "I just realized again that you have a girlfriend."

"No one's used to me having a girlfriend."

"I want two points for using the word 'discomfiture' correctly in a sentence."

"Points granted," I murmured.

"I've changed my mind," she said.

"That was quick. Figures I'd set your personal record."

"No, Special Olympian, I have an addendum. Since I fully expect you to avoid me from now on, can I say one last thing?"

"What?"

"I love you."

TRACK 30

Let's Not Play a LoveGame and Say We Did

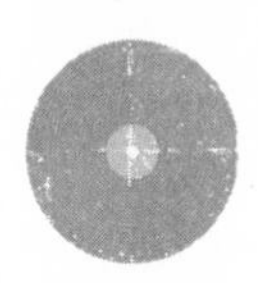

Had Cameo hit her head mid-cartwheel and lost her damn mind?

"Girl Scout Dropout's honor. I love that you scrape your teeth on your fork when you eat spaghetti. I love that you talk too much and get IBS of the mouth when you're anxious. I love listening to you find different ways to pronounce my name. Cam-o-mile. Cam-e-hooo, she's a vegetarian. Cam-e-yo MTV raps. The simple yet effective Meo. Well, Cam-illa Parker Bowles freaking loves you."

I just gawked at her, surely finding new ways to make my face look surgically irreparable in the process.

"Cam—"

"Stop," she said. "And don't you dare say thank you. Think about it. I don't expect anything. Just take it for what it is and try not to analyze away the meaning yet, because I do mean it."

I stared at the living room clock in amazement. Cameo

and I pouring out our guts had taken a mere ten minutes. We'd resumed our spots in front of the TV, and she was calling her mother again, the phone pressed up to her ear. My mom was in her room, still talking to Keith—although it sounded more like fighting tonight, which was atypical for them in a way I didn't feel like caring about. If the honeymoon was over, then so be it, and Stupid Cupid could send Alice to the moon while he was at it.

I heard Cam confirm that her mother was on her way, and I took a swig of my Mountain Dew in relief. She might be gone before Caroline arrived. My tennis baby still hadn't texted me back.

From the sound of their conversation, Mrs. Parnell was feeling bad for missing her daughter's calls and Cam was capitalizing.

"I'm taking you on a school-skipping guilt trip for two to the mall tomorrow, Mother," she said, smiling at me. "I need a Homecoming dress, in case I find a date. Yes, Wade and I broke up. I also need a break from geometry, Mr. Salyers, his lisp, and the coffee breath that accompanies it."

I laughed. When Cam hung up with a chirpy "tootles," I told her about what happened in Ms. Lambert's class between Mike and me.

"Describe the look on his face afterward again," she said.

I did so, adding, "Ms. Lambert is making me write a blog as my punishment."

"Oh, great," Cam said. "Another blog."

"Exactly what I said."

Cameo placed her finger to her temple. "No, I actually

think it's a good idea. For reals. You're a great writer, willing to take risks, so why not put your hit-or-miss jokes to good use? I'll lend you some from my arsenal, too, if you promise to use them wisely."

"Seriously, though," I said. "Do you have any ideas on what I should write about?"

"Just talk about stuff that's happening at school, about stupid crap you and I have done. Wait, I know! I'll wrangle up a few free tickets to the Homecoming Game from President Rottencrotch, and you can hold a contest."

"How is the Homecoming Game going to entice people to read my blog?"

"Shut up," she said. "And don't even think about trying to skip out this year. Your sister is queen."

"I already have my excuse prepared."

"No one cares about your IBS. You're going."

"I'm not."

"We'll see," she said. "Back to the blog. The contest . . . OMG, what about Feetplane? The pairing that stays airborne the longest wins."

Feetplane was another throwback game from our middle-school days. It went something like this: I would lie on the ground with my knees bent while Cameo balanced herself on my feet, using my hands to help her. She would let go, stay up as long as she could, and I'd try to hide my massive boner when she inevitably fell to the ground.

"One of your dumber ideas," I said.

"You have a better one?"

"No hands?"

"Of course no hands," Cameo said. "This isn't for charity. We're going to need videographic proof from the contestants . . ." A mischievous look crossed over her face.

"What?" I asked.

"And people will need a time to beat. Let's go."

"But Caroline . . ."

"It's Feetplane, Jay, not Pin the Dick on the Cheerleader," Cameo said, walking out into the Florida room to look out the window.

She came back in and announced, "The undeniably sexy air traffic controller says the coast is clear. It will take like two seconds. You're awful."

This was such a bad idea, but it was also the least I could do. The girl had just declared her love for me and hadn't required a response. I dropped to the floor and assumed the position, feet in the air.

"Take your flip-flops off," she said. "I'm not an animal."

I did so, and she climbed on board to the immediate sounds of my laughter.

"Quit it," she said, closing her eyes and trying not to laugh. "I'm going to let go."

Her hands left mine, and she was flying. Damn if I didn't find her hopelessly attractive in that moment, her light blue eyes staring down at me, blond hair obscuring most of her face.

"Is anyone timing this?" I asked.

She started giggling, then I started guffawing, and before I knew it she fell on top of me. I heard the door that led from outside into the Florida room slam, and my head jerked in that direction. There she was, standing in the open doorway:

Caroline, just in time to find Cameo on top of me. So my life was now a *Hannah Montana* episode, an after-school special, a reality show, a cartoon, a Danielle Steel unoriginal, a *Melrose Place* soap opera, and—the latest—a predictably bad sitcom. C-line stared at us for a moment, not saying anything, looking more sad than angry. Then calmly walked away.

TRACK 31

Every Melrose Place Has Its Thorn

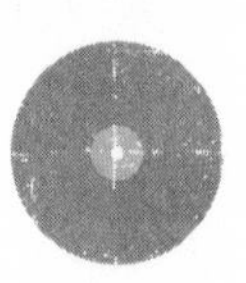

"Caroline, wait!" I shouted, sounding like a parody.

Cameo rolled off of me, and I ran out the door in pursuit of Caroline—figuring she would be gone in about two seconds. Long gone. I ran through the Florida room and leapt off the stairs onto the sidewalk. But she was too fast and already in the car, her hand pressed against her face to obscure my view. Her dad drove away.

Frantically, I reached in my pocket for my phone and sent her a textplanation: "Not what it looked like. I know that's what guilty people say, but it really wasn't. Why would I try to hook up with Cameo when I knew you were coming over? Feetplane is a legitimate . . . never mind. Please come back and let me explain."

When I walked back into the living room, Cameo was sitting on the couch. She'd grabbed a fresh MD from the fridge and was holding it up to me.

"First aid," she said.

"Did that really just happen?" I asked, taking the can from her hand and sitting down.

"It did," she said. "I'm sorry, Jay. It's all my fault. I'm such a hussy. I always knew I'd be the victim of an unintentionally slutty moment."

"It's not your fault at all," I said. "I did this. I'm the one making Caroline insecure about our relationship."

Buzz, buzz. I looked at my screen. Thank God. She'd texted me back.

Caroline wrote, "It's fine, Jay. We both rushed into this relationship before we were ready. I have some things I need to take care of now. No hard feelings."

My heart dropped to my offending bare feet. Caroline was supposed to tell me what was up with her tonight; instead, she'd been treated to the sight of Cameo up against my crotch. I was such an idiot.

Mrs. Parnell honked her horn a few minutes later. Cam left, promising to help me remedy the situation.

I sat on the floor and thought for a moment. I was definitely the dopey Ross in this sitcom, but who was my Rachel, the girl I was meant to be with? Cameo was, of course, my first love. But then Caroline had come along and shown me there was an easier way to do U+Me=Us Calculus, and it didn't involve the hefty amounts of mind-game-playing drama included in the Cameo equation. With Caroline came the game of tennis, her father, and whatever problem had been ailing her recently. I texted her again, asking if I could call. And then I called her anyway. No answer.

Down the hall, Mom emerged from her room. She'd changed into a pair of faded designer jeans and a tight black sweater, her sunglasses holding back her hair.

"Where's Cam, Buckwheat?" she asked distractedly.

"Her mom picked her up," I said. "She was pretty eager to start on her geometry homework."

"And Caroline?"

Guilt, guilt, guilt.

"Her dad put the nix on her coming over tonight," I lied.

"I really do feel for that girl," Mom said, shifting awkwardly in her high-heel boots.

"What's up, Mom?"

"Weeeell," she said, "since you had company, I was going to meet Keith for a drink at Eddie's, but . . ."

Thinking it would be nice to be alone, I said, "It's cool, Mom. Go. Have a good time. Leave me a twenty for a pizza from somewhere else."

"You sure you'll be okay?" she asked.

I should have asked her the same question.

"Yep," I said instead.

"I'll be home in a little bit. Don't stay up too late."

I was guessing that was smarmy Mom code for "don't wait up," but I'd made enough presumptions tonight.

Later, I couldn't sleep. Sheep with Cameo's face kept jumping over my mind's defenses and bleating, "I love you." Then Ms. Lambert's face would appear: *"Want to know which one I think you should date? NEITHER!"* Then Caroline's. But she was a silent lamb.

The next morning, just before I stepped in the shower, I heard Mom walk in the door. Sketchy. I took the scrambled eggs she made directly to the face, swallowing the vitamin she handed me. Then she dropped me off at school in the now-wrinkled black shirt she'd worn to Eddie's. I didn't press her for details. My mind was on Caroline, and Mom needed to save the iron in her One A Day for Abby tonight.

Wednesday evening, in the car with Abby on our way to Mom's, I couldn't help but tell her about Cam's admission o' love, the subsequent Feetplane crash, and the wreckage that Caroline witnessed. I had a big mouth and no one to share it with at school that day. Cameo had been at the mall, Caroline was absent and still not answering my texts, and Ms. Lambert had left me alone during fifth period so she could tend to yet another "class adviser issue." Someone had blown up pictures of couples scoring in the biblical sense and stapled them all over the "We Scored Again and We Liked It" Homecoming float, which provided me with my only LOL of the day. At least it was a loud one.

"That is such a classic girl move," Abby said.

My sister was a homicidal Chatty Cathy right now, veering dangerously close to the median then back toward the gravelly edge of the road. The Homecoming Court picture had come out in the newspaper today, which had put her in a happy place for tonight's reunion.

"What do you mean?" I asked.

"I love you now, Jay, because you're unavailable and I'm

without a warm body to show off my contorted Lady Gag Me–inspired moves to," Abby said in a helium-filled tone. "Can't you see how manipulative she is being?"

I shrugged my shoulders, saying, "I can't read her pa-pa-pa-poker face."

"Of course you can't!" she cried toward the sunroof. "You've showed your cards already! You're such a . . . guy!"

"That I am."

Abby narrowly missed slamming into a gaggle of geese crossing the road. She rolled her window down and screamed obscenities at them as we whirred by.

"I was trying to hit them," she said.

"No need to defend yourself."

Abby shook her head. "It's kind of desperate, but at least Cameo is going after what she wants. Seems like Caroline is too busy being mysterious to care much about your stupid Feetplane explanation. Why does everything have to be so cryptic?"

"I have no idea what either of them wants," I admitted.

"What do you want?" she asked.

"I dunno."

"Maybe you should have figured that out before you got yourself into this situation."

"Thank you, hindsight," I said. "Your after-the-fact observations sure are useful."

I could hear Beyoncé pushing her vibrato through the airwaves.

"Hurry up and put a promise ring on it, if you like one of them," Abby said. "Why should I have to watch those girls mope around school forever because you can't make up your mind? I don't have time to feel sorry for anyone else but you and me."

All Queen Bees should be so kind.

As we pulled up behind Mom's SUV, I said, "Please be on your least offensive behavior. I think Mom and Keith are having problems."

"Tragic."

"She's chillin' in Holiday Shores, Abby. Promise me you won't stick an ice cube in her shirt when she's already down, okay?"

That's what I didn't get about Mike Hibbard's hatred toward me. It never waned. I had more hope for my sister than that.

"Whatever," Abby said quietly.

"I'm not asking you to give each other mani-pedis and spell out messages on the Ouija board. Just dinner. Two hours."

TRACK 32

Sweet Home, Ali Baba Must Have Raided the Place

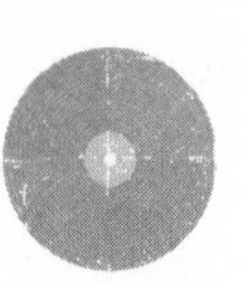

Abby and I walked inside to discover Mom's trailer a hot, marinated mess. The glass door of her china cabinet lay shattered on the carpet; empty packs of Nicorette covered the coffee table. It smelled like the inside of a McDonald's bag—the one sitting underneath the TV.

Mom had yet to greet us, which worried me. I called out her name. No response.

"This place smells like your ass," Abby said, sounding a bit apprehensive.

I turned right, patting my for-now innocent butt as I headed into the kitchen. The good thing about a trailer—number one of one—was that there wasn't much ground to cover in search of Mom.

The kitchen was worse. Dark brown soil, shards of pottery, and bamboo shoots littered the tile floor. The counters were wet and smelled of evaporating beer. And there she was—the victim, the culprit, or maybe both—sitting in the chair farthest from the entryway.

Mom looked certifiable. The worst I'd seen her since our midnight showing of *Marley & Me* a few months ago. Speaking of dogs, a scraggly Lhasa apso appeared to have taken up residence on her head. Tears rimmed her eyelids; corresponding mascara marks streaked her cheeks. Scarier yet, the look on her face: vacant. I wasn't sure if she'd even heard the door or, for that matter, me calling her name.

"Mom?"

She was catatonic.

Abby walked into the kitchen. "What the hell?" Then she saw her. "Mom!"

No response.

"Mom!" she said louder.

At its full volume, Abby's voice could split Mount Kiliman-preferably-Keith-o in half. Her third attempt finally knocked Mom out of her trance.

"My kidlets," Mom said meekly, shaking her head as if to clear it. "Thanks for coming over."

"What in the world happened since this morning, Mom?" I asked. "Are you okay?"

"God, I don't even have supper started," she said, skipping over the question. "We were going to have beef and noodles, Abby. Your favorite."

She said the last part more to herself than to my sister. Abby obviously knew what her own favorite was: nothing. *Oh, Mom. You always get that wrong.*

"That's okay," Abby said softly. "Not really hungry. We need to clean this up."

Abby opened the closet door and pulled out a broom and dustpan. I started wiping down the counters.

"Guys, just leave it," Mom said. "This place is such a shit-hole, anyway."

Abby and I couldn't help but laugh at how matter-of-factly she said it. Mom soon joined in. All three of us, the same cadence, reunited after all of the destruction.

"Look at it," Mom said, throwing her hands out. "I'm officially trailer trash. Who could blame you guys for not wanting to come over here?"

Abby carefully scoped out the perimeter, looking for more pieces of shattered pottery—happy to have a purpose, I gathered.

"What happened, Mom?" she asked, flipping over the contents of the dustpan into the trash can.

"Keith and I had a fight," she said. "It's over."

What do you say when your mom tells you she's stopped seeing the Some Dude loser she cheated on your dad with? And she's upset about it? Comfort her? Celebrate good times, c'mon? Carpe diem and make good use of your "I told you so" opportunity?

"Why?" I asked, not wanting to find out the answer this time.

"He was cheating on me," she said. "Keith left Eddie's last night with another woman."

Abby and I froze, surprised by her bluntness.

"With Brenda, our hair lady, Jay," Mom said, laughing and

pointing to her Lhasa apso 'do. "As you can see, that back-stabber got to me in more ways than one."

"Me, too," I said.

"I'm so disappointed in myself," Mom continued. "Keith was fun, carefree, just wanted to have a good time. And I fell for it like a teenager—no offense. He runs a DUI taxi service, for Christ's sake. What did I expect? Nothing good can come of a relationship like that, especially for a forty-four-year-old woman. Forty-four! And I look old, don't I? Just say it. I'm the picture before the makeover."

"You don't look old, Mom," I said.

"Yes, I do. And now, not only am I haggard, I'm the town joke. And I don't have any food for my kids. Oh, my God, I'm Old Mother Hubbard."

"Mom, you're being retarded," Abby said, finally.

But she didn't sound angry. There was a granule of compassion within her rebuke that I hadn't heard in years from Abby when speaking to Mom.

"Who cares what everyone thinks?" Abby continued. "They'll find someone else to talk about next week. You can help spur the new topic along. Just whisper in a few old biddies' ears at Whereabouts Town tomorrow and you'll be yesterday's *Us Weekly*."

"Yeah," I said, "tell 'em Abby's preggers with Eric's baby. I'll add a 'Bump Watch' feature to the blog Ms. Lambert is making me write."

Abby brushed at my hair with the bristles of the broom, the style she left behind no doubt an improvement.

"Thanks, you two," Mom said, taking a deep breath and trying to compose herself. "You're right. This too shall pass."

Then her face fell, shoulders slumping. Looked like it was passing back over.

"I just have to say this," she said, waving her hand in the air like Mariah Carey searching for a high note. "I need to be honest with you, regardless of how silly and desperate it makes me look."

"What is it?" Abby said.

"I still love your dad," Mom said, starting to cry again. "I always will, and I want you kids to know that."

Abby stopped sweeping; Mom rubbed her eyes, forcing herself to continue.

"I'm not just saying this because Keith and I are finished," she said. "I made a mistake, and I don't think Jim will ever forgive me. I'll never get him back, even though that's all I want. He's too proud, your father. Everyone was talking about Alice Hudson at Whereabouts this week. He's moved on, and I don't know if I ever will."

She was sobbing now, shaking, hands covering her face, and no longer able to speak.

Abby might have predicted this would happen, but not even she could have anticipated the effect of seeing our mother in such a bewildered state. She dropped the broom and sat down on the chair beside Mom. She placed her arms around the sides of Mom's heaving torso, head on her hunched back. Her dark hair spilled over the Lhasa apso.

"I made a mistake, I made a mistake," Mom whispered.

"It's okay, Mom," Abby murmured into her vertebrae, a few tears spilling down her cheeks.

Not sure if I should interrupt their moment, I went over and sat on the floor beside them. "Mom," I said eventually, "who threw the bamboo?"

I had some DUI-mobile tires to slash if Keith was the Kung Fu Panda.

"I broke everything," she said. "I thought it was so cute when he brought it over a week ago and said, 'You've been bamboozled, pie.' Ugh, talk about a bad omen. But my warped mind transformed those shoots into a dozen roses."

"I'm just happy you woke up and smelled them before eloping or something," I said.

Maybe I'd buy her a bouquet, though. With Dad's money. I was so broke.

"And Dad does still love you, Mom," I added. "He told me the other night."

I probably shouldn't have said that, but the hope that instantly appeared on her face made me feel otherwise. I swear I saw it flash across Abby's face, too.

Later that night, I awoke on the floor. I looked around. My groggy brain said, Living room, absurdly late, go back to sleep. Abby's head was slumped over the recliner's armrest, three blankets arranged carelessly across her lap, feet exposed. Mom was on the couch, clothed in her Technicolor dream robe, legs arranged in some kind of weird yoga pretzel shape. Two of her five blankets had fallen by the wayside. Mt. Mommy and Mt. Sissy: I crawled over to fix what threatened their respective nighttime warmth.

Earlier that night, after we'd composed ourselves and cleaned up, the three of us managed to have a pretty good time. Abby agreed to stay overnight, so we gorged on pizza from Amore's Grease-a-ria while watching bad movies. Until two a.m. There wasn't much evidence left of our evening, the pizza box on the counter being all but empty. Only a piece of Mom's crust had survived, because, at Abby's encouragement, she'd dropped it into the humidifier as "an offering to Zeus." She'd had a few beers.

The TV screen flickered, and at a low volume Julia Roberts said to Hugh Grant, "I'm also just a girl, standing in front of a boy, asking him to love her." Happy ending Not(ting Hill)withstanding, that scene seemed a bit masochistic for our tired lot, so I located the remote and pressed the power button before falling back asleep.

TRACK 33

American Girls Are Obsessed with *American Idol*

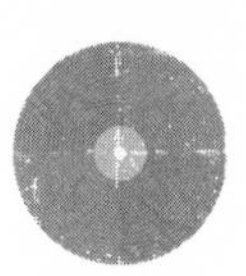

In class the next day, Ms. Lambert was jabbering on and on about Supreme Court Justices and Sandra Day O'Snoozer. Exhausted from the night before, I could hardly keep my eyelids open. She was in an unfavorable mood, though—had already handed out two detentions to wayward board followers, long-suffering Jennifer being one—and I didn't want to test her patience today. Caroline's continued silence and second straight absence from school was the only thing on my mind aside from my parents and—who else?—Cameo, who'd grabbed my arm in the hallway before government to tell me she knew about the Mom/Keith/Hair Girl Brenda situation and we should talk ASAP.

The bell rang ten minutes later, and I couldn't wait to . . . zzzzzz. My head was down when a lacquered fingernail flicked it to get my attention. Ms. Lambert stood in front of my desk, arms folded.

"You can't nap here today, Snuffleupagus," she said. "I have my semiannual evaluation in Principal Boyer's office—where I tell him how much I love my students for a half hour and try to keep a straight face. It's going to be pain-to-the-ful."

Principal Boyer was a fossil, a Crypt Keeper, age unknown. I was certain she could clear the cobwebs from his face long enough to convince him of her teaching aptitude.

"You'll be fine," I said, putting my head back down.

"Go to lunch," she said.

I complained through my arms: "Why can't I stay in here unsupervised, like always?"

"Because I don't have to give you a reason," she said. "I noticed your favorite chicken patty sandwich is on the menu today. What did you call it during the debate? Oh, yes: *an institution*. Yikes. Anyway, go eat your institution and don't miss me too much."

I missed someone else.

"Have you heard anything about Caroline?" I asked Ms. Lambert.

"Have you written your blog yet?" came her tight-lipped response. "Go to lunch."

"I know you know something."

"I know everything."

"I'm going to sneak back in here while you're gone and polish off your Teddy Grahams," I empty-threatened.

"Too late!" she cried. "I already did."

I was late to lunch, and the line for the chicken fatty platter and/or beef strokemeoff was a never-ending story. When I finally emerged with patty in tow, I spotted an empty chair at my old table, where Jennifer, Greg, Sangria, and yes, a happy-looking Cameo Appearance Parnell were seated as usual. Cameo saw me, smiled, and pointed to it. I took a deep breath and walked slowly toward her, thinking to myself that I couldn't—wouldn't—avoid this issue like she claimed I always did. I could confront this. Even with the latest development in Keith and Kim's capricious relationship, even if Cam knew she loved me and I wasn't sure what I wanted, she'd been my friend for years. All I had to do was sit down and be one to her.

"Pardon me, sweetie," I said to her, momentarily British, "is this seaty available for me to park my gray poopin' ass on?"

"Please don't take a dump and run—I'm saving it for Zac Efron," she said, batting her eyelashes. "Just kidding. I suppose I'll have to settle for a Chace Crawford look-alike. A country bumpkin like me can't be too picky about her man-bangs."

"You've been hanging out with Rottencrotch too much," I said, sitting down to the sound of her quick laughter.

Before I could chew my first bite, her head whipped toward mine.

"I love you," she said heatedly, blue eyes staring me down.

"Uhhhhh," I garbled through a mouthful of sandwich.

"Kidding!" she said. "Don't get your man-panties in a wad."

"Ahhhhh!"

"Don't deny. I've seen your underwear drawer. Briefs galore. Man-panties to go along with your man-bangs."

"I haven't worn man-panties since the seventh grade," I said, swallowing. "I've graduated to . . . absolutely nothing."

"Oh, the humanity!" she exclaimed, laughing again.

Such a familiar, comforting sound. Maybe falling back into our old rhythm would be easier than I thought.

"So your dad and my mom—"

But she cut me off. "Can you guys give us a minute?" she asked Jennifer, Greg, and Sangria.

Once they'd relocated to an adjacent table, Cameo said, "Up-Her-End-A Brenda strikes again. At least you and your family can unhitch yourselves from the Parnell DUI-mobile."

How had I missed that now-obvious note of emotion in her voice for so long? Oh, yeah—I'd been too busy worrying about myself.

"How did you find out?" I asked.

"Dad came home *Chelsea Lately* last night, and I was upstairs practicing piano. He told me everything, which was surprisingly better than nothing."

"Are you okay?"

"I'm used to it," she said, grabbing three fries and shoving them into my mouth.

I chewed and swallowed, looking meaningfully at Cam.

"Please tell me that look on your face has nothing to do with sympathy and everything to do with diarrhea. I did declare my love for you to the sound of crickets a few nights ago, and if you start pitying me, I'll be the most pathetic girl this side of the Mason-Dixon."

"Albeit one with a more marketable *American Idol* back-story," I offered.

"You have my attention," she said, resting her chin on her palm. "Keep talking."

"When are they holding auditions?" I asked.

"As of ten thirty-three this morning, they haven't been posted on the Web site."

"Well, I don't care when or where they are—we're going. We'll bunk at a Worst Western if need be."

"What if you're with Caroline?" she asked.

Cam was implying, "What if you don't choose me?" And assuming that Caroline would be speaking to me again.

"If C-line and I are together at that point, then she'll have to deal with it."

"Puh-lease, Jay," Cameo said, waving her hand dismissively. "Don't try to be a hard-ass."

"Really didn't fit, did it?" I said, smiling.

"So you'll seriously go with me?" she asked in that flirty way that still drove my shiz crazy.

"Sure."

She let forth a dolphin squeal and grabbed my hand, then suddenly a cry rang out from nearby: *"Gaaaaaay Baker!"*

I couldn't quite make out the words at first, or maybe I was in denial.

"Gaaaaaay Baker!"

And there was my confirmation, a different voice this time. I looked to Cameo. "Is this actually happening?"

She nodded, dropping my hand and looking around the cafeteria.

"Gaaaaaay Baker!"

She turned back to me. "Mike's table."

It didn't take a genius. A riptide of rage surged through me; the kind of blood-pressure tsunami only the Herp could provoke.

"Do you want me to go over there and give him a piece of this?" she asked, rolling her eyes after she realized what she'd said.

"That's okay, Cam. I guess it really is time to harden my ass."

TRACK 34

Viva la Chicken Patty!

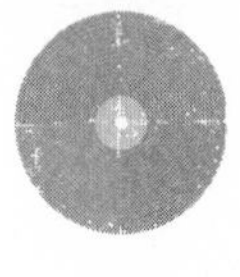

I moved my head around Cameo and saw Mike's entire Massengillian round table laughing with their heads down, apparently thinking that if a *Gay Baker*–yelling culprit couldn't be identified, Ms. Riddell—the lunchroom attendant—would have no way to inflict her special brand of schoolmarm punishment. I spotted her talking in the adjacent teachers' lounge, and thus far she hadn't noticed the ruckus.

Another shot to my heterosexuality rang out: *"Gaaaaaay Baker!"*

That one was particularly loud, the words sounding as though they'd been emitted from Mike's snout.

I stood up and yelled, "Notorious P.I.G.!"

I could see parts of his big fat face oozing over the nook of his elbow: cheeks turning their windburned red with laughter, beady eyes watering in enjoyment. I grabbed my greasy patty from its bun and shoved it behind my back.

"Paging Notorious P.I.G.!" I shouted again. *"Please report to the lobby. Your mom is here to whack it for you."*

As much as he might have preferred a punishment-free sneak attack, Mike Hibbard couldn't ignore a comment about his mom in front of the entire cafeteria—a Technical Knockout (TKO) as my dad had taught me so many years ago when we'd don gloves and box playfully, him on his knees and me jabbing ineffectively. I hadn't even realized he'd been training me in case I found myself in a fight someday. Like today?

Mike's head rose from the table, and he turned around to grill me hatefully. I quietly apologized to the patty for what I was about to use it for: ammo! In an instant, I brought it around from behind my back and whipped it in his direction, letting the processed-meat puck fly.

All those hours spent on the tennis court had sharpened my aim, and the patty connected directly with Mike's forehead. The impact caused the crumbly crust to splatter in a million different directions, a few stray meat chunks landing on top of his Supercuts flattop.

RIP, JFK, but I wished Zapruder or someone else had been there to film the messy carnage. It was magnificent. And the mortified look on Mike's face was the Rice Krispies Treat topper of my dreams. Sprinkles of satisfaction snapped, crackled, and popped their way through my veins, filling me with the kind of empowering adrenaline that could only lead to more problems. I felt like I could do anything. I was a chicken-patty-wielding juggernaut.

The entire lunchroom erupted in laughter. Even Mike's own table of sheep joined in sheepishly, proof that it was a physical impossibility not to lose it when someone was so blatantly victimized by food.

Mike wiped the patty from his face in disgust, grabbing the stray chunks in his hair with his football-fumbling hands and dramatically throwing them to the ground. Then he moved fast—maybe faster than he ever had—springing from his chair, marching in my direction, and looking all kinds of ridiculous. Rather than stand there laughing merrily and awaiting my fate, my fight-or-flight-o-meter told me to bravely meet him in the middle.

We reached the median clearing between our tables at the same time and promptly jumped each other, almost as if we were doing a chest bump like those weird Bryan twins did in celebration after winning a tennis point. Mike Hibbard and I were a low-budget Doublemint commercial. Something more minty, even. Mentos.

As we homoerotically fell to the ground, I thanked Sir Isaac Newton I had more forward momentum than he did. I landed on top and began sucker-punching his cushiony gut, knocking the wind out of him. Literally. A sharp fart rang out from his dumb-ass, a rank bonus to the indignity he was already suffering. More laughter, every person in the room rapt by what was transpiring. Except for one.

I felt a strong tug at my shirt collar. Not thinking, I turned around to see who was interrupting my moment of glory. Ms. Riddell stared down at me, eyes bugging out.

Mike made the most of the distraction, and his fist connected with the right side of my face. Pain reverberated down my cheekbone. His take-back had been stymied by his positioning, but the punch was still forceful enough to push my neck back toward Ms. Riddell.

Ms. Riddell found a better grip on my collar, jerking me upright with both her hands before Mike could strike again. I kicked him on my way up. I'd stung like Manny "Pac Man" Pacquiao, now I was floating like Madame Butterfly against my will.

Someone must have alerted Mr. Ellington to the commotion, because he appeared out of nowhere to haul Mike's wide load off the floor. Together, they escorted us to the principal's office, the cafeteria cheering as we exited.

In one final act of Tom and Jerry foolery, I raised my right arm to claim the victory. Mr. Ellington roughly shoved it back down with his free hand, and it hurt.

"You idiots will be lucky if you're not expelled," he said.

I hadn't thought of that.

Ms. Lambert was in Old Principal Boyer's crypt when we walked in and interrupted her evaluation. Neither party looked surprised to see us, which was living, breathing (barely, in Principal Boyer's case) confirmation as to how fast good news traveled.

Self-proclaimed victory or no, my adrenaline high started to wear off as I realized my actions were about to meet their consequences.

Ms. Lambert surprised me by speaking first, but I should have known. She was born to meddle heavily.

"I've already discussed this matter with Principal Boyer," she said grimly. "He's going to let me have a turn with you two before exacting your final punishment."

Mr. Boyer mumbled an incomprehensible rejoinder through chapped lips, but I thought it better not to ask if he needed an IV. Known to expel students for transgressions far more benign than ours (e.g., respected bathroom graffiti artist Jake Troyer), the man did not take kindly to having his rickety boat rocked.

As angry as she looked, Mike and Ike had a better shot at survival with Ms. Lambert.

TRACK 35

Family Affair to Remember to Forget

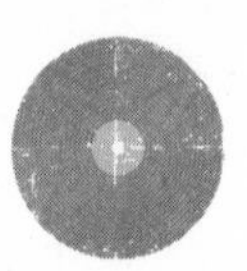

"I *knew* something this catastrophic would happen," Ms. Lambert said, grabbing a few chocolate Teddy Grahams from her top drawer and popping them into her mouth with a defiant glare in my direction.

The Teddy Graham–hoarding fabricator had lied about the depletion of her supply, but I said nothing. We were back in her classroom, Mike and I positioned at desks as far away from each other as possible—me holding an ice pack against my right cheek. A silent Ms. Riddell stood sentry against the closed door.

"Luckily for you two," Ms. Lambert said, chewing loudly, "I blame myself a little for exacerbating the problem and then leaving its resolution to chance for so long."

She sighed, rearranging the bloodred scarf/altar cloth that hung around her neck.

"Tsk, tsk, tsk. Thinking a freshman class debate was a good

idea. I was so excited. I thought you both could handle it. Ha! When will I learn that freshman boys have the collective maturity level of a doobie-smoking sea monkey?"

Ms. Lambert had plundered that sea monkey reference from me. I wanted credit, and I ached to point out the logistical complications of underwater pot smoking, but I kept quiet. I knew she was testing me. She expected more from me than Mike. Expected more from me than *this*. I'd let her down again.

"So here's what I'm going to do," she continued. "I'm going to give you a chance to air your dirty laundry in front of me—a mediator who doesn't get paid nearly enough to sort through your crap, but maybe I'll get a commemorative plaque or something. If I feel satisfied that a permanent resolution has been reached, I'll see about coaxing Principal Boyer into decreasing your punishment. *Comprende?*"

Mike and I remained silent, nodding our heads.

"Fancy that, no superfluous talking from either of you yet," she said. "Maybe you're smarter than a fifth-grader, after all . . . but probably not."

Ms. Riddell nodded her head in agreement with the latter half of that statement.

"Why does this keep happening, Jay?" Ms. Lambert asked, turning to me first again.

"It's pretty simple," I said. "First Mike comes at me with some lame variation of how gay I am, then I retaliate with an equally hackneyed joke about how fat and stupid he is. Family-unfriendly mayhem ensues."

Mike sneered. "Don't forget the disrespectful comments about my mother."

"He's right," I said. "How could I forget about Mike's mom? I usually don't like to leave her out."

"Yo momma jokes," Ms. Lambert scoffed. "How subtle of you."

"And sticking porn in my locker and screaming 'Gay Baker!' in front of the entire cafeteria are revolutionizing the bully industry? At least I didn't go for the jugular outright, like he did."

"You're a paradigm of virtue, Jay," Ms. Lambert said.

"In that case, did I mention that he started it?"

"Quiet," she warned. "This is my show, not yours."

"Back in seventh grade," I said, undeterred. "I have no idea why. Maybe you should ask him."

Ms. Riddell came over and put a hand on my shoulder.

"Okay, sorry," I said, raising my left hand in the air. "I'm done."

"Transparently self-serving as it was," Ms. Lambert said, turning to Mike, "Jay made a decent point. You seem to be dropping some seriously narrow-minded atomic bombs in his direction, Truman, and with little regard for the consequences. I've asked your counterpart this question before: what beef with Jay could be worth staking your entire academic career over? And, yes, Jay, I heard the unintentional pun. Shut up your face."

"Yeah, right," Mike said sarcastically. "Like I'm gonna spill it in front of Jay. Either way, we're suspended. What's the point?"

"If you want your cleats to touch the football field again, you'll start talking. Mr. Ellington owes me a favor for telling him why his quarterback sneak wasn't fooling anyone but his own team."

Some turbulent indecision danced across Mike's face. On one hand, he loved sucking at football; on the other, he didn't want to reveal the inner douche inside his bag.

"What's going on, Mike?" Ms. Lambert asked, more gently this time. "Why did you start it?"

"Fine. You *really* want to know? Because Jay's slut mother screwed my father two years ago, and my parents got divorced because of it. And she just screwed him again the other night."

Oh, c'maawn! Finally, things were getting better with Mom: She was being honest with me, Abby had forgiven her, and there was a modicum of hope for her marriage. Come to find out Old Mother Hubbard was sleeping with Fat Father Hibbard? The same woman who'd just bawled her eyes out over *my* father? I couldn't believe it, and I didn't. Mike Hibbard, the Fartman villain of this comic book, didn't need a tragic origin to explain away his behavior.

Ms. Lambert remained calm—probably anticipating the root of the problem would be a flame-broiled Whopper.

"That's quite an accusation, Mike," she said evenly.

"It's true," he said. "And the truth hurts when your mom is a whore."

Ms. Riddell walked over to Mike, whispered something into his ear, and he sat up straighter.

No, no, no, I chanted inside my head. My mom had made a mistake or two, but no way had she hooked up with Mike's dad.

"I've seen your dad, Mike—" I blurted out.

"Stop right there, Jay," Ms. Lambert demanded.

"I should be able to defend my mom."

"You'll have your turn. Mike," she said, "if this were a court of law, here would be the part where you provided some evidence to corroborate your accusation."

Mike thought for a moment and said, "If you say so. I found an e-mail from Jay's mom on my dad's computer . . ."

Even Jadakiss would find this "evidence" to be Ludacris. Mom was a notorious spam artist who e-mailed Whereabouts Town flyers to anyone with a faint broadband connection.

"He found an e-mail!" I cried. "Guilty! Lock her in the slut tank—"

Ms. Lambert threw her stuffed gavel at me. It grazed my ear, and I stopped talking.

"Listen before you react," she said. "Go on, Mike."

"Back in seventh grade. My parents weren't home. Mom was visiting my aunt; Dad was out late again. I was bored, my laptop died, so I went down to the den to use Dad's. He must have forgotten to sign out of his account. The e-mail was there when I turned on the screen."

I ground my teeth together as Mike continued.

"I forwarded it to my e-mail address, showed it to my mom, Dad admitted to the affair, and they got a divorce. I couldn't do anything about it—couldn't tell anyone without embarrassing my family. So I took it out on Jay, I guess."

"This is so asinine," I said, unable to keep quiet any longer. "We're supposed to believe this Judy Blume backwash?"

"And there's the other reason I hate this kid," Mike said, pointing at me and looking at Ms. Lambert. "He thinks he has it all figured out, but he doesn't know jack."

"I'm holding an ice pack up to my face right now, about to be suspended for making you fart. I'm aware all my cylinders aren't firing."

"Can I show you the e-mail on my phone, Ms. Lambert?" Mike asked.

"Absolutely. My confiscation numbers are a little low this month."

"Take it. Enjoy. I don't freaking care anymore."

Ms. Riddell walked over and took the phone from Mike, delivering it to Ms. Lambert. Her eyes scanned the screen for several minutes, and then she looked directly into my eyes, nodding her confirmation.

"I'm sorry, Jay," she said.

No, no, no.

"So what now, dude?" I said, looking at Mike. "You have a DNA sample?"

"No, but your mom left her black aviators at my house."

"What brand?" I asked, choking on the words.

"Ray-Ban," Mike said. "They thought I was sleeping when they walked in. Your mom's laugh is so annoying."

"What *specific* night did she leave them there?" I asked him.

"Two nights ago."

There it was, the Scooby Doo coup de grâce that proved Mom's guilt once and for all. Tuesday, the night I'd scared off

Caroline, Mom had gone off to Eddie's wearing her sunglasses. That morning, in the car on our way to school, she couldn't find that pair or any others.

Mom had lied—or omitted part of the truth, at the very least—to Abby and me. Again. But more important, did Dad know about her second affair?

TRACK 36

Gossip Girl You Know It's True

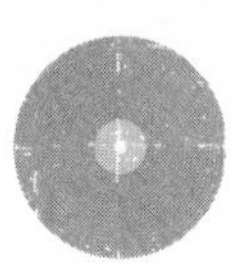

Everyone gave me some time to process the unwelcome news, possibly because I was shaking a little. Embarrassing, yes, but I couldn't stop. Even Mike was respectfully quiet while Ms. Lambert typed furiously on her computer for ten minutes. She began printing off a few documents, then turned her chair around to scrutinize us through her tortoiseshell frames.

"Okay," she said, breaking the silence. "We all know by now that I'm all-knowing, but even I didn't see this one coming. I'd say the circumstances surrounding your fight were *and still are* very touchy, and should be treated as such. Therefore, I'm willing to stick my neck on the line and speak to Principal Boyer on your behalf. I wore this nifty scarf today, so I should be fine."

"Thank you, Ms. Lambert," Mike said, visibly relieved.

"I haven't done anything yet," she said, grabbing the printouts and holding them up for us to see. "I'm going to need you both to sign this; we'll call it the *Gossip Girl* Contract. In it, I've laid out the terms and conditions of your parole. Ms. Riddell, would you be kind enough to hand these gentlemen their agreements? These witch boots are killing me."

Ms. Riddell brought over my contract, and I started reading.

> Hey, y'all! It's Gossip Girl. I'm going to need you two cupcakes of joy to read the following items carefully and sign at the bottom. Please note that if you don't adhere to all of these mandates for the remainder of the school year—and believe me, I'll hear about your violation—then you'll be resentenced to serve a more appropriate suspension (or expulsion) of my choosing. I'm very persuasive. Principal Boyer is my great-uncle. Ain't that a trip? Unfortunately, you can't tell anyone (see Item 1 below). XOXO—GG
>
> **Item 1.** Outside of your parents, you shan't speak a word of what we've discussed here today to anyone. This includes sisters, girlfriends, boyfriends, Facebook harlots, dissociative identities, et al. Cameo Appearance Parnell is particularly off-limits, Jay. I'm bitter about the Katy Perry float, and I'm positive she's responsible.

Item 2. Only you can understand what the other young man in this room is going through. Therefore, by code of this contract, it's official: you're friends. Yay!

Item 3. Don't think I've forgotten that you can lead an immature horse to water but . . . blah, blah. This is how I'm making you drink. Mike: Jay has a blog due to me on Friday. I'm feeling generous, so he now has until Monday, and guess who gets to help provide him with material? I hear you're good at it (e.g., the porn you placed in his locker). For the remainder of the year, twice weekly, you will send Jay an e-mail containing two hundred and fifty useful words on a mutually agreed upon topic. Jay: You will collaborate with Mike on this effort and not be a jackass. You both will include your e-mail addresses under the signature line of this contract, and I'll verify that they're valid. If they aren't, I'll hunt your real ones down and filibuster them before suspending/expelling your lying . . . I'm getting a bit carried away here. Power trip!

Item 4. You will put a "P.S. I love you" at the end of each e-mail, telling the recipient something nice about himself. Ahem, you will not use off-color irony. (Example: "That gay shirt you were wearing today would look really good on your mom. Hardy-har-har.") Consider this my long overdue

> moratorium on any/all homophobic, Oedipal, and farm-animal-related nastygrams. I'll be asking you to cc me at random, because you can't be trusted. Let's practice what I'm preaching. Once you've signed, please turn to the other person and apologize.

"Feel free to sign in blood," Ms. Lambert said when Mike and I had finished reading. She was clearly pleased with herself.

We both signed and handed the contracts back to Ms. Riddell.

"I'm sorry, Jay," Mike said finally, turning to me with actual empathy in his eyes. "And believe it or not, I'm jealous of you and Caroline. She seems pretty awesome."

Ack. Leave it to Mike to inadvertently pick a sore subject when trying to make amends.

"It's cool," I said. "I'm sorry, too. My sister's boyfriend, Eric, said you're a good football player, for whatever that's worth."

"Congratulations, children," Ms. Lambert said. "You're one step closer to becoming America's Next Top BFF's. I'll go tend to Uncle Boyer."

About ten minutes later, Ms. Lambert came back and informed us that she'd convinced Principal Boyer to knock down our sentence to a two-day suspension. It could have been a lot worse: an expulsion-turned-ITT-Tech-enrollment kind of disaster. Signed contract notwithstanding, I was grateful to Ms. Lambert for the reprieve.

"Thank you, Ms. Lambert," I said.

"You're very welcome," she said sincerely.

Then she had Mike and me call our parents. Obviously, I chose to contact Dad, who didn't sound pleased when I told him why I needed a ride home early.

Mike's dad arrived first, and Ms. Riddell escorted him out of the building, leaving Ms. Lambert and me alone for a minute.

"Are you okay, Jay?"

"What am I going to do?"

"Nothing," she said firmly. "You're going to go home, sit down at that MacBook you're always talking about, write your blog, and let your parents figure out their own lives."

"I'm not even sure if my dad knows about my mom and Mike's dad."

"I'm sure your mom will tell him," she said. "And if not, you can cross that bridge when you come to it. With my guidance, of course."

My phone buzzed and a text from Dad appeared on the screen.

"That's my ride," I said.

Ms. Lambert walked me out, mercifully taking the emergency exit route to avoid my seeing as many other students as possible.

She opened the door for me.

"Why are you going to all this trouble for us?" I asked before walking through.

"Let's just say my parents went through a pretty nasty divorce, and I know how it feels. See you Tuesday."

"So the blog . . ."

"Is still due Monday," she said. "Peace be with you."

"And not so with you."

TRACK 37

Sitting, Waiting, Wishing I Was Somewhere Else

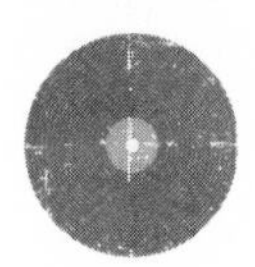

As soon as we took off in his Cadillac, Dad began reading me the riot act. I took my five minutes of fatherly reprimands like a champ, though, and his docile nature soon returned.

Funny, but he couldn't help but ask, "How did the punches feel when you landed them?"

"Scarcely any pain," I said. "Thanks to our boxing sessions. Kind of like punching a waterbed."

"Why didn't you go for his face?"

"I couldn't distinguish it from his other body parts."

Dad shot me *the look*.

"I felt weird about it."

"I'm glad," he said. "I want you to be able to defend yourself, not shove a bone into someone's brain."

"Graphic."

"Fighting often is," he said sternly. "Never again unless you absolutely have to."

"Okay," I promised.

He was quiet for a minute, and my thoughts turned back to the latest Mom-capade. Did Dad know about affair number two?

"Dad?"

"Yeah?"

"Do you know Mike's dad very well?"

I watched his face closely for any clues. Saw nothing.

"Sure," he said. "I sold a pretty big policy to him a while back. Nice guy, so try not to punch his kid in the gut anymore, okay? It's bad for business."

He laughed, and I pretended to laugh. Confirmed. Dad didn't know Mom was doing enough biznasty with Mr. Hibbard for the both of them.

For some reason, Dad parked in the driveway instead of our three-car garage. He never took Abby's spot, and he'd filled Mom's with a few boxes of crap, but his should have been available. Let it go, Jay.

We stepped through the front door into the house, and the smell of cheese immediately pervaded my nostrils. Ominous sizzling noises crackled from the stove. Someone was cooking in the kitchen.

"My client is making us lunch."

"Great," I said, smiling wanly.

I was hungry enough to eat the stray patty chunks off the cafeteria floor, but I didn't have the energy to pretend to enjoy another one of Alice's nasteroles. Garage mystery solved, though: Dad must have let her park in his spot, which sure did eliminate the walk of shame—not that Sleeping Buffy cared what Alice looked like post-coitus.

I braced myself, walked around the corner, and discovered the person who stood facing the stove wasn't Alice. She was a bit shorter, her figure trim but more womanly. Wavy blond hair cascaded down her shoulders, and a pair of black Ray-Ban aviators sat atop her head.

I might have told Cameo I was getting used to life's *banzai!* moments, but nothing could have prepared me for the sight of Mom back in our house, flipping grilled-cheese sandwiches for my father and me.

Mom turned around, spatula in hand, a wry smile on her face.

"I assume you want Tater Tots with your sandwich, Mr. Holyfield," she said.

Hell, yeah, I did. But I had a few other things I wanted from her, too—starting with an explanation.

"What are you doing here?"

Dad sat down at the bar. "Is that any way to greet the person cooking your lunch?"

"Sorry, Mom. I wasn't expecting you, that's all."

"It's okay," she said, turning back around. "I can understand why you'd be surprised. I came over to talk to your dad this morning."

"Interesting . . ."

"Lunch is almost ready," she said. "Why don't we take our plates into the living room and have a powwow about your fight today."

Not yet. I needed time to figure out what was going on.

"Dad and I already talked about it," I said. "Can't I just eat and take a nap? It's been a long day, and we didn't get much sleep last night, Mom."

"It won't take long," she said. "Plus, we have to discuss your punishment."

Was she serious with that motherly talk? I was supposed to take orders from her, the woman who left her aviators at Mike Hibbard's house?

Dad and I went into the living room, him sitting on one couch, me on the other. Mom brought in our food and set it on the coffee table. She handed me a Mountain Dew, and I fully expected her to sit down beside me or on the recliner. But she sat next to Dad.

"So tell me what happened, Jay," Mom said, biting into her sandwich.

"Mike called me gay, I hit him with a chicken patty, we jumped each other, I punched him, he farted. It was a once-in-a-lifetime opportunity, so I punched him again. He punched me. We're suspended for two days. I laughed, I cried, I hurled. The end."

Even though she could have taken issue with my tone, Mom didn't—patience actually was one of her virtues. Instead, she launched into a five-minute spiel on the dangers of fighting and how "there's nothing wrong with being gay, not that I'm saying you are," etc. She capped it off with this little morsel of wizdumb: "All that being said, the social game isn't easy. I remember what life was like as a teenager. Hard."

Then she looked at Dad and smiled. He smiled back. Holy

reconcilable differences, what had they been talking about before I showed up? Had Mom told Dad she knew he still loved her? Had Dad forgiven her? Were they . . . getting back together?

"You're really lucky your suspension wasn't more severe, Jay," Mom continued, sighing. "Please tell me you've seen the error of your ways."

"I've seen the light, Mom, promise. Ready to show me the punishment?"

"You want the good news or the bad news first?" Dad asked.

"Bad."

"You're grounded for two months."

I could have sworn I said bad news. Grounding me from leaving home was like grounding Buffy from leaving her bed.

"The good news is your mom will be around more during your house arrest."

Mom was beaming—radiating the kind of happiness I hadn't seen from her in years. She must have told Dad how she really felt about him—that it was over with Keith. Maybe she'd even attempted to bring up Mr. Hibbard but Dad had stopped her, wanting to focus only on the fact that he still loved her. Maybe I was living in a dream world, but who was I to condemn theirs?

"I'm not moving back in or anything yet," Mom clarified. "But your dad and I are going to see where things take us."

Sure, part of me wanted to say something right then to end the charade, but the other part of me—the part that wanted my family back together—urged me to keep mum about Mom. This was everything I'd wanted to happen these last two months, and all under false pretenses. No idea what to do, I ate my Tater Tots quietly and sat there like a turd.

TRACK 38

Heads Caroline, Tails Cameo

I finished eating and I asked my parents if I could take a nap. "Unconsciousness seems like a better alternative for me today," I explained, trying to sound as normal as possible. They agreed, and I actually did fall asleep until around the time school ended.

I awoke to the sound of my phone buzzing Cameo's name.

I answered, whispering, "I'm grounded and my parents forgot to take away my cell. Text me which part of the fight you liked best: the patty to the face or the subsequent farting."

"You got it!" she said, hanging up.

As much as I would have loved to tell her what was going on with my parents, what had happened in Ms. Lambert's classroom, and why my suspension was only for two days, I knew I couldn't. Ms. Lambert would be sniffing around Cameo's bungholio every day hence, to see if I'd deposited any information.

"Mark me down for the fart," Cameo texted. "Everyone is

talking about what happened, and I gotta say, Jay, I think you won! You should write about this in your blog. Title it: One Small Toot for Mankind. Or maybe include a multiple-choice question on what the fart smelled like?"

"I'm not really allowed to talk about what happened with anyone. They could extend my suspension."

And everyone knew the answer was beef strokemeoff.

Cameo: "Bummer. But I understand. I've gotta go watch Katie Tracey wrap her cottage-cheese thighs around our Homecoming halftime dance. It's gonna be a spectacle and a half."

"Bright side: The crowd will finally know who moved their cheese," I wrote.

"Not if I convince her to keep her warm-up pants on," she texted back. "P.S. I don't care if you're grounded, I'm picking you up next Friday and YOU'RE GOING to the game. Baby Jesus told me to immediately delete your next text because he knows it's going to be negative. Besides, I have a present for you. You'll like it."

With everything else going on, I'd forgotten about the C-lizzle/Cam-e-rizzle/Gay-bizzle love triangle for approximately three hours—a personal best. But now I couldn't help wondering if Cameo's present was a trip for two to the Love Shack. Wait, Caroline. It was Thursday, and she hadn't answered her cell since Tuesday night at Mom's. Where was she? What if... I just called her house phone and asked Crazy Daddy Richardson?

I stared at my cell, trying to work up the courage. My mom's voice popped into my head: *"It doesn't hurt as much if you rip off the Band-Aid, Jay."* I exited the confines of my bedroom and checked the living room and kitchen for any signs of my parents. They were gone—for now. I shut my door and placed the call before I could change my mind, saving the "Band-Aid" for after the conversation when I'd need it to cover my brand-new asshole.

Mr. Richardson answered on the first ring.

"Hello?" he said accusingly.

"Hello, Mr. Richardson. How are you?"

Silence.

"It's Jay."

"Thanks for the refresher, Jay, but I recognize your voice."

"Perfect," I said. "Look, Mr. Richardson, I'm sorry for the other night."

"What happened the other night?"

Of course Caroline hadn't told him about Cameo and me; revenge wasn't her kind of dish.

"Nothing," I said. "I played really badly."

"What else is new?"

"Well, I was curious if Caroline is available?"

"She's not."

"Oh."

"Anything else?"

"Well, I just, I . . ."

"Spit it out, Jay. I'm on my way . . . somewhere."

Dammit. I just wanted to talk to Caroline, make sure she was okay, finally give her the chance to talk. I felt like I was going to burst, like any minute the emotion would come pouring out of me and into the ear of the one person in the world least likely to care.

"I, uuuuh"—sniff—"I really need to, uh . . ."

"What's wrong with you, son?" Mr. Richardson asked, but his voice was softer.

"I don't know if Caroline told you anything about my parents—"

"She told me enough," he said. "They sound like a couple of nightmares."

"Then I won't bore you with the details, only to say they're at it again. I really care about your daughter, and I'd like to talk to her. Can you tell me what's going on? Why hasn't she been in school the past few days?"

Mr. Richardson sighed, apparently gauging how much down-low he should upload.

Finally, he said, "This stays between us, you hear?"

"You have my word."

"I don't give a flying donkey about your word," he said. "I'll have your ass if this gets out."

"Sure, that too," I said—Cameo's line.

"Caroline's mom is having some issues."

"I thought she was in the Philippines."

"A few weeks ago, Mrs. Richardson came back to live with us on a trial basis. I didn't want Caroline to say anything to you, or anyone, in case her mom fell off the wagon again. That's why we moved to Indian Lake in the first place. Her mom not only fell off the wagon last year, she got back up and drove it into a tree. A lot of people in town were talking after the accident. It distracted Caroline, and she started performing unacceptably as a result. You know better than anyone I won't have that; my little girl is too talented, too special to join Andrea Jaeger in the convent or Jennifer Capriati in rehab."

"With all due respect, sir," I said, "why'd you relocate to Indian Lake? This place is a tennis black hole."

"I'd rather drive Caroline where she needs to go than have her immersed in all that petty drama. Plus, Indian Lake is within driving distance of some froufrou rehab facility that I knew would come in handy if my wife ever decided to come back and mess up again."

"Empty Promises?" I asked.

"Second Promises," he said. "But yes. For once one of your little nicknames is appropriate. They specialize in patient/child rehabilitation and wasting my money. But they have a tennis court, so I allowed Caroline to move in with her mom for ten days while she undergoes treatment. They take away all cell phones, so Caroline's is here and she won't be back until next Saturday. Quit calling and waking me up. I can't figure out how to turn off her ringer."

So that was why she wasn't responding to me. Poor C-line.

"Thanks for filling me in, Mr. Richardson," I said. "Would you tell Caroline I said hello, if you see her?"

"Sure," he said. "I'm on my way there now."

"Thank you."

"Not so fast, son," he said. "Have you been practicing?"

"Huh?"

"I didn't spend all that time on the court with you for my

health," he said. "You need to keep your limited skills sharp for the tennis tournament at Maple Lane next month."

"Uh, sir, I don't know if tennis is really my thing—"

"I don't know if I really care," he said. "You're doing it."

"I'll mark my calend—"

He had hung up.

TRACK 39

I'M LIKE A JAYBIRD, I'LL ONLY BLOG AWAY

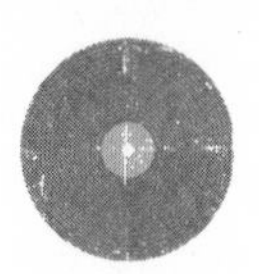

Thinking of Caroline—probably doing some kind of trust-building exercise with her mom right now—I walked over to my desk and opened Alba MacBook. Checking my e-mail, I found a message from footballfreak7490@yahoo.com (Mike).

> Hey, Jay—
>
> Since Ms. Lambert has a thing for Gossip Girl (I've cc'd her on this e-mail), I figured you could use a little inside info for your blog. A lot of crap gets talked about in the locker room. People might be interested in reading some of it. See below.
>
> Mike
>
> P.S. The *Roe v. Wade* comment was a good one. I figured I'd get the baby taken care of while we're suspended.

I laughed, remembering the days when Mike used to be funny. Another e-mail popped into my inbox a few minutes later. From Ms. Lambert, it said simply:

> Mwahahaha! This is good stuff, Mike. Disclaimer: Unless you're writing something nice (yeah, right), no proper names, Jay! We're not adding a libel suit to your recent crime spree.

I e-mailed Mike a thank-you, asking for his approval to use a certain tongue-in-cheek title for his section of the blog. Then I gave him props for finding the most disgusting penis on the Internet for his porn surprise.

When Mike e-mailed me his okay a half hour later, I was immersed in the creation of the blog and having a cathartic experience or something.

There was a perfunctory knock on the door, and Abby barged in, looking perplexed. Or was it perturbed? Did she know about Mom and Dad's potential reconciliation? And what about the most recent addition to Mom's prime-time schedule?

"I have two questions for you," she said, sitting down on my bed and pulling her dark hair into a ponytail.

"Yes, I ate all the candy from your Homecoming Queen gift basket. No, I don't know where Eric's missing chromosome is."

"Shut it. How much does Eric need to torture Mike next week?"

"It's fine," I said. "Call off the horn-dog. I think Mike and I are done with our reindeer games for now. Next question?"

"Why are our parents sitting in the hot tub together and grossing me the F out?"

Aw, shiitake, they were removing clothing already. This wasn't good. I looked at Abby, struggling to deny the urge to tell her everything then and there. Contract or no contract, my sister deserved to know; I would take my licks from Ms. Lambert's chops if need be.

But then, almost smiling, Abby said, "At least I won't look like Little Orphan Annie walking down the field at Homecoming next week. I told Mom she could walk with Dad and me."

Yeah, okay. What kind of person would put the kibosh on a girl experiencing her crowning achievement with both parents by her side—free from thoughts of Some Dude Named Keith and Mike's unsightly dad? An honest one, I supposed, but I didn't care.

"Alice, we hardly knew ye," I said.

"Who?" Abby said.

"I need help with my blog," I said, turning back around to my MacBook.

"No."

"Please, Abby. You just updated your Facebook status to 'In brother's room, text responses may slow down accordingly.' You know more about this stuff than I do."

"Fine. But I want my own Dear Abby advice column."

"Done. 'Ask Queen Beeyotch.' I'm sure it will be my most popular feature."

For the next two hours, Abby took over my bed and answered questions about her section of the blog. I made use of Mike's e-mail for another section and also texted back and forth with Cameo re: a third feature. The final product read like this:

The Edumacation of Jay Baker (Volume I)

About the Blogfather

Jay Baker here: fifteen-year-old freshtard and brotherly afterthought of this year's ILHS Homecoming Queen, Abby Baker. Text 4955 for her cell number; you won't get it, but you'll receive Fresh-blog! notifications and a joke of the day, like this one I just made up: What portable device can a nerd utilize as both a computer and a female body part substitute? A Pocket PC. *Cymbals crashing*

As everyone trapped on our Animal Farm knows, ILHS isn't exactly a barnyard of excitement. Our motto: What happens in Indian Lake stays . . . the same. So sometimes we have to turn on our generators and create our own Orwellian entertainment, whether that be by signing up for Boot Scootin' Boogie line-dancing classes, taking advantage of Subway's extended late-night hours, or scavenging through the Dumpster behind Taco Bell for bong materials. Not that our fine citizens would ever dream of smoking pot or anything . . . when they can eat it in their brownies.

Anyweed, my hope is that *Edumacation* makes our little armpit of the world a smidgen less malodorous . . . so sit back in your uncomfortable IKEA futon, sync your iPod, grab the hand of someone you love to hate, and feast your eyes on a blog where klass has been dismissed indefinitely.

I Bribed Gossip Girl, and She Told Me the Following

The cost of living in NYC is astronomical, of course, but who knew the mysterious star of *Gossip Girl* would be forced to relocate to Planet Ohio? Recently, I caught up with her inside the Indian Lake Rollarena, slipped a twenty into her purse (which she insisted on calling her "eTrade account"), and she gave me the 4-1-1 faster than a speeding mullet (fluttering behind a male Russian figure skater).

"Spotted: Two freshman wrongs not making (out) a right in the Rollarena bathroom. As Joey Butterfinger placed his lips against Amy

Fish-Filet's face, I almost threw up the McRib I'd just eaten. What would their parents think? Who cares? These two should be shipped back to Long Island where they came from. XOXO and all that crap."

Gossip Girl may not be as eloquent as she once was, but life at the Rollarena changes a person. She started hawking up a few other rumors, but then she had to run—mentioning something about her dad kicking her off their Family Share Plan. Will GG have enough minutes to continue gossiping? Will Joey Butterfinger break off more breading than he bargained for with Amy Fish-Filet? I dunno. You'll have to log in tomorrow to find out.

Ask Queen Beeyotch

Taking your cousin to Homecoming? Posting another personal on craigslist? Considering attending the latest "model search ~~scam~~ convention" to come through town? Don't act yet. For a limited time only—until she graduates—ILHS's resident Queen Beeyotch, Abby Baker, is taking a break from basking in the warm glow of her own fabulosity (and the tanning bed) to field questions related to your inability to buy a clue and get a life. All hail the Queen at the e-mail address linked above; what do you have to lose by sending her a "Q"—except your fashion-backward headband?

Your Royal Beeyotchiness:

I see you struttin' yo Stove Top Stuffin' around our school, and, giiiiirl, you got it goin' on. How do I get people to notice me like they noticin' you?
Hamburger Help-Me

DEAR HAMBURGER HELP-ME:

You can start by subtracting two tablespoons of creepiness from your personal recipe. Unfortunately, if you're trying to be me, it's not going to happen. Wikipedia calls it a monarchy for a reason. My suggestion for you is to do some after-class soul-searching and find your niche. A few questions you may want to ask yourself:

1. Are you good at sports? Ms. Riddell is always recruiting bottom-heavy femmes fatales for the softball team.
2. Do you Excel at anything related to Microsoft Office? Perhaps you can make *The Laker Log* look more like a yearbook and less like someone's unfinished scrapbooking club project.
3. Do you enjoy grooming animals? Some socially awkward girls really seem to enjoy intramural horseback riding.

Bottom line: Spend some time outside my shadow to find out what makes you specifically original, not generically unpopular.
Queen Beeyotch

Classroom Suicide Watch

Teachers of Indian Lake High School, you're on 9-1-1-notice. Fellow students, if you know of a faculty member whose lectures are the equivalent of verbal NyQuil, just shoot me (an e-mail) and regurgitate your story. You're not alone in the fight against fatal boredom.

This week's victim comes to us mentally battered and bruised at the hands of Mr. Pi R^2 and his geometry class. Because this dilating pupil is currently carrying a C, she wishes to remain anonymous.

Jay: Can you tell our readers about what you've been experiencing in Mr. Pi R^2's class?

Anonymous: Do you know that feeling you get when you stand up too quickly—the blood rushes to your head, and you feel like you're about to die? That's what I feel like when he starts talking.

Jay: Want to mention any specific lectures?

Anonymous: The one on the Pythagorean theorem. When he started making hypotenuse jokes like "Hypoten *use* the side opposite the right angle," I wanted to jam my protractor into my soul.

JAY: I kind of liked that one. Don't you think you're being a little dramatic?

ANONYMOUS: A+B=Can't do it anymore.

JAY: It might have helped if you'd copied down the right formula.

ANONYMOUS: Obviously, his teaching methods are ineffective.

JAY: Anything you want to say to your fellow classmates?

ANONYMOUS: If you're sitting in the front row, wear a visor—unless you want to join his gleek club. Oh, and we are the world, we are the children. That's all.

HAVE YOU SEEN THIS GIRL . . . PLAY TENNIS?

For those of you unfamiliar with the game of tennis, I encourage you to come out to Maple Lane Tennis Club next month—not only to watch me make a mockery out of the boys' tournament, but to stand back and marvel as Caroline Richardson lays the smack down on the girls' draw. Just gathering up a little school spirit in advance. RSVP within the week for a chance to win two free tickets to the Homecoming Game next Friday. The drawing will be next

Thursday, and I'll throw in a free *Sports Illustrated* football phone if I like the winner. In the meantime, I'm sending out this long-distance dedication—a song I wrote for Caroline. . . .

SWEET C-LINE
(SUNG TO THE TUNE OF
NEIL DIAMOND'S "SWEET CAROLINE")

Met on the court,
You looked cute in your skort.
Too bad I couldn't hit the ball.
Was in the fall
That I became your beau.
Who'da believed you'd stoop that low?
Lips, touchin' lips,
Makin' out, touchin' me, touchin' you.

Sweet C-line (I miss you),
High school never seemed so good.
I've been inclined
To believe it really would
Alwaaaays blow.

Look at my texts—
They're from my parents only.
Wish you'd send one or maybe two.
And when I blog
Hurtin' runs off my keyboard

And how can I tweet when missin' you?
Bird, touchin' worm,
Freakin' out, killin' me, not-eatin' you.

Sweet C-line (come home soon),
My tennis game is not so good.
I've since declined (shanks galore)
Since you left my robin hood.
Oh, no, no.

Abby and I were in her room now. She was sitting on her bed with Alba MacBook in her lap, reading over my tripe before posting it on Blogger for me. I fully expected her to poke fun any minute, so I'd dragged Lazzie down to the floor with me as collateral; vulgar acts performed on stuffed animals weren't above me.

Once finished, Abby lifted her eyes from the screen and stared at the wall.

"What?" I said. "Too Perez Hilton?"

"No," she said, annoyed. "Would you quit putting yourself down all the time? You know this is good. Our school will freak over it."

"Then why are you still staring at that unfortunate senior picture of Eric on a Jet Ski?"

"I have a hard time saying nice things to your face."

I was having a hard time containing my excitement, not only because I was trying to play it cool below Abby, who'd finally validated something of mine from the pedestal I put her on, but because she was right: I knew the blog was decent, and I felt a weird sense of pride about it.

"What's up with the Caroline part?" Abby asked.

"I wanted to do something nice for her," I said. "She's been through a lot lately."

"What about Cameo?"

"She's got a present in store for me."

"I'm sure she does. Quit yanking her around and make a decision."

"Yank this," I said. "I can't *wrap it up* until I see Caroline and talk to her."

"Whatever," Abby said. "When is Caroline coming back?"

"Next Saturday. We should do some tandem bike riding to make this week go faster."

"I think I just pulled my hamstring on purpose."

TRACK 40

I'M COMING, HOMECOMING! TO THE PLACE WHERE I DON'T BELONG

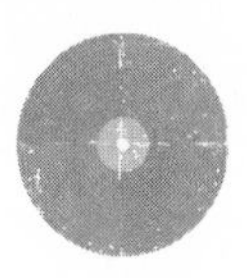

When I returned to ILHS on Tuesday, having honorably served my suspension, it was like walking into *Cheers*—everybody knew my name. Not only were my classmates coming up to tell me which part of the blog they liked best, juniors and seniors were giving me snaps, too.

I had certain people to thank, of course, for taking a chance on an unknown blogger. Baby Jesus, Abby, Mike, Cameo, and Ms. Lambert—the supporting cast behind *Edumacation* had been invaluable.

After Abby had posted the blog last Friday night, she linked it to her Facebook page. All Queen Beeyotch had to say was "read this," and the visitor-tracking device she'd installed climbed from two to two hundred hits in a matter of minutes.

I'd posted entries almost every day since, and Mike had been e-mailing me tips in conjunction. Although we weren't exactly ready to join Brody Jenner and his pointless posse in a circle jerk, our budding bromance was headed in the right direction. We even surreptitiously low-fived each other in the hallway on Wednesday, after a particularly sizzlin' "Gossip Girl." Admittedly a ho-moment, but we were relieved to take our eyes off our broke-backsides. Ms. Lambert continued to watch over us carefully. She was slightly irritated by "Classroom Suicide Watch," but not so much that she made me retract it: "This is what I call poetic justice—Mr. Salyers has been parking his PT Cruiser in my faculty parking spot lately." Then she asked when she was going to be in the blog. Me: "When you start waxing anesthetic about Sandra Day O'Snoozer again." Her: "Get over it before I make you go to lunch, Ginsburg!"

I informed Cameo that Caroline was going through some "Mommy issues," and she immediately understood: "They seem to be going around." Yes, probably better than anyone, the snizzly cheerleading dynamo understood. She didn't mention the dedication to Caroline on my blog, though, and I was too much of a cowardly lion (pussy) to bring it up. She was more disappointed by my omission of the Feetplane contest, but I placated her with the promise of a future plug for the annual cheerleading competition held in January that no one cared about. Things between us were back to normal, but only so much could be said until Caroline returned, so we kept our exchanges pretty surface. For once, Cameo didn't appear in a big hurry to wrangle up a new boyfriend—even with the Homecoming Dance on Saturday, which she pledged to attend alone.

My parents continued to confound me. Mom had come over a few nights for dinner, and she and Dad appeared to be taking it slowly. What was her angle? Her plan? She hadn't stayed over yet, although they'd gone hot-tubbing a couple more times. Nothing a few chemicals couldn't kill.

Every time I'd attempt to bring up Mom's most recent tryst in conversations with Dad or Abby, something would suddenly come up, Greg Brady–style, and I'd run back into the kiddie pool. I'd remember my sister wanting both parents to walk her down the field on Friday, or Mom in her trailer crying and wondering if she'd be alone forever, or me—trying to keep it together while cooking a Betty Cracked-Out imitation of her spaghetti.

One night, when Mom wasn't there, I started to tell Dad but then switched topics, asking whatever came of his two-second dalliance with "Alice Doesn't Cook Here Anymore." He said she'd been fine with ending it—referencing her strength and independence with the same look of admiration he'd had on his face the night we played basketball. Seemed eons ago. Belatedly, I felt bad for Alice, the stranger who'd offered to cart my ass to and from the tennis club for no reason other than how pathetic I must have looked. She was an innocent bystander to the big card-house of lies that had become my home.

I needed an outsider's opinion on what—if anything—I should do, but obtaining one obviously had its logistical (and contractual) complications. Ms. Lambert was watching, and the only advice she would offer was "Give them a chance to sort things out and write your blog, gummy bear!" The one person I could tell without immediate ramifications—the person who had kept her secret so well from me—would be home on Saturday. And I sure hoped C-line would talk to me.

It was Friday. Unbeknownst to my parents and my sister, I'd agreed to let Cameo pick me up for the Homecoming Game. To show my gratitude for her blog assistance, I wanted to surprise Abby, who'd written me off this morning on our way to school. She'd asked me if I was going, and I'd clutched my stomach and commenced with the fart noises, denoting what I could unleash if thrust into an unfamiliar social setting.

I was waiting outside my house for Cameo and her mom when the black Lexus pulled into the driveway a half hour later than expected. Eliza Doolittle was in the driver's seat, the passenger side empty—Mrs. Parnell nowhere to be found.

I opened the door and stepped into the car.

"Buckle up, we're tardy for the party," she said, smiling at me. "Sorry."

Cameo was looking as sumptuous as ever in her cheerleading uniform, and the sight of her still made my neck hair stand up.

"Long time, no see, Eliza. You're looking quite bangable this evening."

"Thanks, love!" she said. "Hair toss!"

Her pom-pom of hair was tied up in ribbons for the game, so she couldn't toss it. Instead, she rolled her neck in some sort of impromptu dance move, which then turned into an entire voguing series.

"Carrie Ann Inaba?!" I cried.

"Ten!" Cam said.

"Len Goodman?!" she beckoned.

"Nine," I said drily.

Cam pretended to be offended and began backing out of the driveway. As I turned around to make sure she didn't nail the basketball hoop, I noticed the human waste of space curled up and passed out in the backseat. What was it with the Parnells and their backseat hijinks?

I turned back around to Cam. "Do I need to ask why Marilyn Monroe isn't driving?"

"Poor Mother started to," Cam explained, "and she was doing really well until she ran over our neighbor's dressed-up goose statue. I figured Eliza better take over before she harmed any more innocent pottery in her Mother's Little Helper bender."

Somebody FedEx Mrs. Parnell to rehab with Caroline's mom. I didn't ask about Some Dude Named Keith, what his excuse was, because there really wasn't one big enough for him. And he would probably mistake that thought for a compliment. Poor Cameo.

"Was the goose wearing a bonnet?" I asked.

"Let's segue into another topic," Cam suggested. "How are things with your parents now that Keith is vagazzling Brenda?"

"Next," I said.

We were silent for a few minutes as Cameo sped down the highway with ease.

"Cheer up, Cameoke," I said. "I heard something on the radio the other day about a local Search for a Star contest. Know anything about that?"

"Already entered," she said, nodding her head enthusiastically. "First prize is an all-expenses-paid trip to an *American Idol* audition this summer. What are the odds?"

"We're there," I said. "I'll customize a T-shirt with your sepia-tone Facebook profile picture on it. You're going to do this, Cam."

"Spirit-fingers crossed," she said, glancing back to check on her mom. "I have to get out of this town ASAP. That's a Carrie Underwood song, actually."

We hit a red light, and Cameo grabbed her iPod—finding and playing the song.

"I have an idea on how we can ensure your success," I said. "I just need to ask the person first."

"I know about Alba MacBook and her Googling powers, Jay," Cam said. "You can refer to her by name."

"Not Alba," I said, laughing. "Alba knows how to please her masturbator, but I'm talking about someone who knows more than Oprah."

"I've always wanted to meet Kathy Griffin!"

We arrived at the school five minutes before kickoff. Cameo put the car in park and turned to me. "Kiss me, loser," she said.

"What?" I said, laughing nervously.

"I'm serious."

"What kind of present is this?" I asked.

"Just do it!" she demanded. "On the lips. No tongue. Softly. I'm a girl, not a freezepop."

Cam was so adamant that I had no choice but to do as I was told. She closed her eyes, and I brought my lips forward, touching hers. Confused about where to go from there, neither of us moved, frozen in time. Finally, Cameo pulled back, turned off the car, and jumped out. I followed suit and barely managed to catch the keys she threw at me.

"Where are you going?" I asked dumbly.

"I needed to be on the field five minutes ago!" she cried, already running toward the stadium. "Make sure you stay past halftime!"

"Should I crack a window for your mom or something?" I called out.

"Sure," she called back. "Sometimes the fresh air revives her."

She already has a breath of fresh air in you, I thought, watching Cam run away.

TRACK 41

Baby Jesus Knows I'm Miserable Now

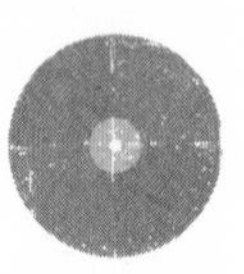

Reluctantly, I walked toward the stadium and took my spot in the admission gate line. So this was a football game? Everyone was decked out in sweatshirts featuring our school's politically incorrect Indian Chief logo, corresponding red and black school colors splashed all over their bodies. I had on my aviator jacket, a polo, faded jeans, and flip-flops.

"Are you a student?" the female gatekeeper asked, implying that I didn't look like one.

No, fiftysomething face-paint lady. Just a fan of really bad football.

"My sister is the Homecoming Queen," I said proudly. "You wouldn't happen to know where Abby Baker is?"

"The Homecoming Court and their parents are underneath that white tent over there," she said, pointing to her left.

"Thanks." I paid and walked over to the structure. The first person I saw inside was Rene Rottencrotch, who'd been named to the Homecoming Court under a swirling stench of controversy. As acting class president, she'd assisted in counting the votes, so tramp-stamp a big VOID on that Ernst & Young result envelope. I didn't see my parents anywhere, but then the crowd parted toward the back of the tent like in a bad teen movie, and I saw Abby, looking more stunning than ever. Her hair was done up in some kind of ringlet-schmabob, and it surrounded her jewel-encrusted crown perfectly. The white suit she wore set off the olive pigment of her skin, another reminder that I would never be "in" with Dad, Abby, and the melanin crowd (but surely "noma" would spot Mom and me soon).

Looking surprised, Abby smiled in my direction, white teeth gleaming.

"Surprise, Sis," I said, walking up to her and bowing slightly.

"Hey there, bubs," she said, actual kindness in her voice. "I can't believe you're here. At a football game."

"Never thought you'd see the day, did you? Objects in your car's mirror aren't as lazy as they appear."

"Nice shirt," she said, reaching out and pointing to my alligator emblem.

"I have a hunch the Lakers are going to take a bite out of the Waynesfield Golden Gophers tonight."

"Uh-huh."

"Where are Mom and Dad?" I asked.

"They're getting me a Diet Coke."

"There's some right over there," I said, pointing to the cooler on the table.

"I want a *fountain pop* from McDonald's," she said. "Dad looked at me like I was a diva, but Mom agreed. You know how she loves her drinks."

"Yes, I know," I said, Mom's secret rearing its ugly head again.

"Kickoff is in thirty seconds."

"Huh?"

"The part where a team kicks the ball and the opposing team catches it, duh."

"I know what 'kickoff' means and you're wrong," I said. "It's the part where the wimpy soccer player gets to play."

"I stand corrected," she said, smiling again.

"I guess I'll go find a seat."

"Jay?"

"Yeah?"

"Thanks for coming."

"No problem."

This was the Baker sibling equivalent to an "I love you, I love you too" moment, and a hug felt appropriate. I held out my arms.

"What is that?" Abby asked.

"The beginnings of a hug."

"Gross," she said, but she extended her arms, too, and we embraced.

I scanned the bleachers for a familiar face, but no one appeared eager to share their Lakers seat cushion with me. Thankfully, I spotted Ms. Lambert sitting beside a kindly-looking man with light blue eyes and a shock of white hair. He wore khaki pants and a crisp button-down with a sweater vest over top of it—a stark contrast to the many layers of black fabric cloaking my favorite teacher. I caught her eye, and she beckoned me forward with one of her long purple fingernails.

"Hello," I said, stepping up to her row and sitting down beside her. "Just proving that I'm not ashamed to be seen with you."

"I'm honored to be the last resort of the school's first blogging sensation," she said. "*Quelle surprise* to see you at a football game. You're becoming quite the man about campus."

"I'm on an undercover assignment," I said. "Extreme football awfulness and its effect on the teen-male ego."

My eyes darted to the dapper gentleman sitting on the other side of Ms. Lambert, and she noticed.

"Jay, this is my husband, Gary Lambert," she said. "Gary, this is Jay Baker. He's a *freshman*, but we're working on it."

Gary and I shook hands, exchanging pleasantries. Then I whispered to Ms. Lambert, "You never mentioned anything about being married to the ghost of Paul Newman."

She whispered back, "You never asked."

"Why go by the ambiguous *Ms.* Lambert, then?"

"An admittedly feeble nod to the feminist movement," she explained. "So, yes, a part of me is going to die when that Katy Perry float comes bouncing down the field during halftime."

"Are you feeling any heart palpitations yet?" I asked, nodding toward the field.

A time-out had been called, and the cheerleaders were performing a thirty-second dance break to 3OH!3's "Don't Trust Me": "Shush, girl, shut your lips. Do the Helen Keller and talk with your hips." Cameo, in particular, was letting her hips do the talking.

"Look at those feminist movements," I said, laughing to myself.

"I wish I'd brought my Nerf gun," Ms. Lambert said.

"Transition. I have an after-school project I need your assistance with, Ms. Lambert."

"I'm busy," she said, shaking her head in disbelief at the cheerleaders.

"I need you to help Cameo like you've been helping me," I persisted. "She hasn't had it so easy on the parental front, either."

Ms. Lambert looked at me like I was crazy. "Oh, silly rabbit. I have boxes of tricks up my sleeve for Cameo."

"She already contributes to my blog."

"The world doesn't revolve around your blogosphere, Jay. I'm talking about Ms. Parnell's singing aspirations. I've heard her decking my hallway with her Gaga outbursts."

I smiled.

"Yeeees," she said, rubbing her hands together. "We're going to start with the girl's poor choice of songs, and fast-forward from there."

"Don't tell me," I said. "You're a classically trained opera singer."

"Oh, because the fat lady has to sing, right?"

"That's awkward."

"Ha! As much as I love making you squirm, this wench's cords haven't touched *The Pirates of Penzance*." Then her voice dropped to a whisper: "I sowed my wild oats as a Vegas lounge singer, before duty called."

"Is 'duty' the gentleman beside you whom I just said howdy to?"

She nodded. "Moving on. I've got connections. Parnell will be fine."

I told Ms. Lambert about Cam's entry into the local singing competition, and our collective wheels spun regarding her try-out song until the referee's whistle sounded, signaling the end of the first half. The male announcer came over the loudspeaker: *"And now, Lakers, it's time to introduce this year's Homecoming Court!"*

He began calling forth the Court, starting with Rotten-crotch. Class by class, the girls and their parents exited the tent, walked down the field, paused for pictures, then got into an awaiting limo.

"Where, exactly, are they going in the limo?" I asked Ms. Lambert.

"On a magical carpet ride around the school and back into the tent the team pitched."

"Were you trying to make that sentence explode with double entendres, or did it just happen naturally?"

"I'm holding you in contempt."

"On what grounds?"

"School grounds."

"Ladies and gentlemen, please give it up for this year's Home-coming Queen, Abby Baker! Abby is accompanied by her parents, Kim and Jim Baker."

And there they were, my family, the Bakers, walking down the football field together. The three of them looked so happy, so proud to be there in front of everyone, and my heart ripped open a bit as I took in the sight: Abby perfect as usual, Dad in the three-button suit he wore so well, Mom beautiful in her flared trousers and suede jacket, blond hair blowing in the breeze. Lord, I loved her. Despite her trespasses, I wanted her in this family. Why did her secret ever have to come out? *Couldn't things just stay like this?*

But then I looked at Dad and Abby again, unknowing participants in a sham, and I knew it had to be done tomorrow, when the dust from Abby's achievement had settled.

I must have had "inner turmoil" written across my forehead, because Ms. Lambert was staring at me now.

"Life really is a fucking bitch," she whispered.

This bold statement catapulted me back down memory lane. I didn't have to go far.

Earlier this week, I was doing homework at the bar, as usual. Mom was cooking—what else?—spaghetti because it was Dad's favorite. Dad arrived home from work and snuck up behind her spot at the stove, hugging her so she would know it was him. "Let me try some of that, Big Momma," he said. "Of course, Big Dad." She grabbed the spoon and arranged the perfect bite for him, bringing it carefully to his dramatically puckered lips. "He's been spoiling his supper since the day we married," she said to me, smiling. Dad swallowed, danced a jig in approval, and summoned her toward the garage for a predinner "smoke-'n'-chew." Mom popped a Nicorette into her mouth, placed the spoon on the tropical-themed ladle rest she'd found on their honeymoon in Jamaica, and said, "I know she won't eat, but will you tell your sister dinner's ready, Buckwheat?" "Sure," I said. They walked out the door together. The tagline to the picture etched on the ceramic surface of the ladle rest: "Life's a Beach."

"Life's a bitch," I said to Ms. Lambert, looking at Mom. "But I know my mom isn't. I need to expedite her explanation."

"You do what you have to do, Jay," Ms. Lambert said. "I think you've given this plotline enough time to unfold. Through the edicts within the Gossip Girl contract, I was trying to teach you that sometimes the best reactions aren't knee-jerk."

"Thanks for helping with everything, Ms. Lambert."

"It's what I do."

Remembering Cameo's request, I forced myself to stay past halftime. Right about when somebody fumbled and somebody else fumbled again, I saw her: my tennis paramour, back a day early from the land of Empty Promises.

TRACK 42

Always Be My Baby Maker

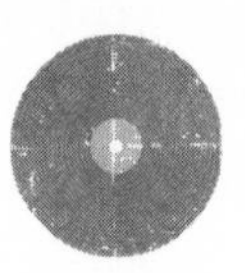

Caroline looked as jizzorgeous as ever: skin glowing, eyes vivid green, wavy brown hair pulled up in a tennis bun. Her expression was serious, and who could double-fault her for that? She'd been through a lot these last nine days, and perhaps she'd regressed to the girl who hadn't smiled those first few weeks of school.

"I have to go," I told Ms. Lambert. "Caroline . . ."

"I see her, Jay," she said. "Try not to do a flying leap off the last stair. I don't think her Miley Cyrus arms are strong enough to catch you."

"You'd be mistaken," I said, bolting down the stairs and rushing to catch up to Caroline. She'd almost reached the concession stand before I could tap her on the shoulder.

"Hey, you," I said, grinning as she turned around.

"Hey, Grasshopper," she said, smiling a little. "I was looking for you. I figured you'd be hiding next to the candy, not watching the game."

I reached out for her, pulling her body toward mine for the biggest hug I'd ever delivered in my life. Her slim limbs fit snugly inside my bag of long bones. I smelled her hair, my inner creeper emerging to inhale every inch of her.

"Are you sniffing me again?" she asked, mouth against my chest.

"Yes."

"Can we go somewhere and talk?"

"Of course," I said, looking around for an isolated location. "What about under the bleachers?"

"I see you haven't changed much since I've been AWOL," she said, breaking the hug.

"No, I actually have. Grasshopper suggests we head over there to that grassy knoll."

"Okay," she agreed.

"But I need a Mountain Dew first."

She looked at me as though I had confirmed her initial reassessment.

"What? The concession stand is on the way."

"How did you know I'd be here?" I asked Caroline.

We were sitting on the ground, staring at the football stadium in the distance.

"Cameo," she said, nary a hint of jealousy in her voice.

"Cameo?"

Hence why she wanted me to stay past halftime. Caroline was my mystery present.

"Yes," she said. "A nice counselor let me check my e-mail on his BlackBerry a few days ago. Cameo sent me a message explaining everything. She admitted that she loves you, but she knows she's not the right person for you. And she thinks, deep down, you know it, too."

"There's something I should tell you right away, then," I said.

"She told me she was going to kiss you one last time."

"No tongue."

"I know. And I also know the rules and regulations of Feet-plane."

"Welcome to the mile-low club," I said, thanking Cameo in my head.

"It's, uh, *interesting* to be here."

There was a reason I'd prolonged my decision while Caroline was away, an explanation for why I hadn't gone for the gusto in the car with Cameo. I liked Caroline now. A lot. Cameo was right. She'd foreseen this plot's conclusion and taken action, taken care of me like she always had. In return, I'd had the balls to steadfastly question her depth. Time to step out of the kiddie pool and unveil my shrinkage.

"I'm sorry about this whole disaster of a situation, Caroline. I haven't really done right by either of you."

Caroline shook her head quickly and smiled. "I already know how you can make it up to her and me."

"How?"

"Take Cameo to the Homecoming Dance tomorrow. She has a dress, she needs a date, and there's no reason for you not to if you're *just friends*."

"I'm grounded," I said, reaching for the first excuse my mind could grab.

"For what?"

"Punching Mike Hibbard in the gut and making him fart."

Caroline laughed and said, "Cameo told me about that, too. An accomplishment, yes, but not a good excuse."

"I have IBS."

"She said to remind you nobody cares about your IBS."

I laughed. "Fine. I'll figure out a way to take Cameo to the dance if it means you'll forgive me. My mom owes me one, anyway."

"What do you mean?"

"I'll tell you later."

"Then it's settled," Caroline said. "Cameo also included a link to your blog in her e-mail."

"How long was this e-mail?"

Caroline ignored me. "I think you're so talented, Jay. And I love the song you wrote for me. Thank you so much."

"You're welcome," I said. "Your dad is right; you are too talented not to be appreciated."

"I don't know about that," she said, smoothing her hair back.

"It's true."

"Enough about me. How've you been?"

"No," I said.

"No?"

"I want to talk more about you first," I explained, and my hand dropped down near hers to squeeze her pinky. "How are you? How's your mom? I thought you were staying at Empty Promises until tomorrow."

"They want to finish up with Mom alone," Caroline said, smoothing back her hair again. "She's doing okay, though. Taking everything in stride. Drinking her wheatgrass shots. She was always a calm person, I guess, but that might have been the Grey Goose. Don't you just love geese?"

"Oh, sure. They're just misunderstood swans."

Caroline smiled, continuing, "She seems more . . . I don't know . . . at peace now? It's weird. You should see my dad, Jay. He cries a lot these days."

"Huh?" I said, wide-eyed.

"Yep," she said. "He needs her, so I hope she can keep herself together."

Caroline had tears in her eyes when she added, "I need her, too."

Not really knowing what to say, I put my hand on her back and began rubbing it. She leaned over and rested her head on my shoulder. I wrapped my arms around her, and we sat there together for a while, thinking about our moms.

"I know you hate it here," she said, sniffling—breaking my heart in the process. "But I kind of like the Lake."

"I'm getting used to its toxicity," I said. "Our kids might have webbed toes, but maybe people will think it's cute."

"Who said anything about babies?" she asked, sounding just a tadpole like her former self.

"You never know."

She kissed my cheek. "Let's focus on your backhand for now."

C-line listened carefully while I told her about my parents. I was uncertain if she noticed the burden leaving my shoulders—or, for that matter, when I started falling in love with her again.

Toward the end of the fourth quarter, Caroline and I rejoined Ms. Lambert and her husband in the bleachers. My teacher and my tennis baby soon ensconced in a girl-talk huddle, I looked out to the field, searching for Cameo. She was on the track, mid-cheer ("A-W-E. S-O-M-E. Awesome! Awesome! To-tal-ly!"), but I caught her eye and mouthed the words "Thank you." A flicker of sadness crossed her pretty face. Then she winked at me. ("Awesome! Awesome! Whoopsie!") She turned around and stuck out her booty, completing her cheerography (yes, according to her, we lived in a cheerocracy). I smiled, knowing she and I were going to be just fine.

Epiblog

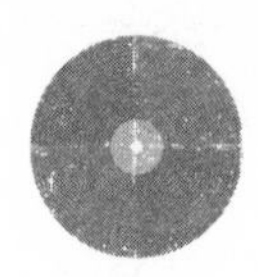

The Edumacation of Jay Baker (Volume 31)

A Blurb for Our Sponsor

The Edumacation of Jay Baker is sponsored in part by Whereabouts Town. Don't hate me because I'm going commercial; I have manscaping fees. My mom recently purchased the venerable used-clothing store from its previous formaldehyde-ready owner, who decided to ~~die in~~ move to Florida. As Mom prepares to franchise Whereabouts Town into neighboring counties, she'll need a catchier slogan than current front-window stalwart "Whereabouts Town are you from?" For you, this means *contest* and a chance for the winner to pick up fifty dollars' worth of not-half-bad vintage clothing. An example: "I went to Whereabouts Town and all I got was this vintage T-shirt." 1, 2, 3, go crazy.

Confronting Mom had gone better than I thought. The day after the Homecoming game, she picked me up and we drove to the bike path. As we power-walked along the water, I *banzai'd!* her and brought up Mike's dad.

"I mean, Jesus, Mom—how many fathers in my school have you had relations with?"

"I've never slept with Mike's dad, Jay."

"I don't want to know the gory . . . what now?"

"How do I put this delicately?" she said, running her fingers roughly through her hair. "It wasn't a home run . . . more like somewhere in between a double and a triple."

"Not a surprise that Mike's dad is a shortstop in the bedroom. That being said, Mom, you still *almost* caught the Herp Senior. Why was *that* even an option?"

"Sam Hibbard and I went to high school together," she said. "He came into the store a few years ago, around the time your dad and I first started talking seriously about divorce. He was someone to talk to. We exchanged e-mail addresses and things got out of hand."

"Until Mike's mom found out?"

"No, I'd put a stop to it before that."

"But are *you* why the Hibbards got divorced?" I asked.

"Partially. They'd been having problems for a long time."

"If Mike's mom knew about it, weren't you worried she'd tell Dad?"

"Terrified."

"Then why didn't you just tell him yourself?"

"I thought about it every day. I'd start to, then I'd talk myself out of it, thinking that would be even more selfish than what I'd done already. I wanted to keep my family together more than anyone. Oh, Jay—I was wrong, of course. Maybe if I'd told your dad then, the whole Keith thing wouldn't... anyway, I'll talk to him today. And I'm so sorry you had to find out the way you did. I take full responsibility for all of it. You are beyond *un*grounded."

(Reverse punishment. Mom took Cameo and me to the dance that night, which wasn't so awful. She danced; I observed.)

"What about last week?" I asked. "You left your aviators at Mike's house."

"I had too much to drink that night, and Mike's dad wouldn't let me drive home and wake you up. I'm glad he didn't. He took me back to his place, and I slept it off in his bed. He made a floor bed, like you always do. Nothing happened."

She went on for a bit before I stopped her. "Okay, Mom. I get it. I forgive you. Can you just be my mom now?"

She started crying, took her aviators off, and looked directly into my eyes. "Oh, honey. Absolutely."

In their bedroom with the door shut, Mom told Dad that same day. I knew because I listened outside of it, just as I had a few months ago. There wasn't much else for them to hide at that point, so I pretty much heard the whole conversation. They didn't fight, really; more like detachedly exchanged information.

I was in the living room watching TV when Mom emerged a half hour later, shutting the door behind her.

"Take care of your father, Buckwheat," she said, hugging me closely.

A disheveled-looking Dad appeared in the living room shortly after she left, beckoning Buffy and me into the garage for a smoke.

"We're getting a divorce," he said, taking a puff.

"I figured."

"Sorry about all this, Jay."

"For what? You didn't do anything."

"I played my part," he admitted. "And I really should have protected you and Abby more."

I shrugged for his benefit. "We looked out for each other during your sabbatical. You can't be all things to all people, Dad."

"I can try. I know you'll miss having your mom around. And I will, too. I think it's just . . . too late for us."

I looked at my conflicted father. "Not that you need my permission, Dad, but it's okay for you to let Mom go."

He swallowed hard. "Thanks, buddy."

Dad headed toward Buffy's treat box, throwing three biscuits near her immobile body, and then I grabbed the basketball.

"P-I-G?" I asked.

"You bet," he said, shuffling his boat shoes in a surprisingly intimidating gesture.

A few weeks later, Dad started seeing Alice again, and Mom bought Whereabouts Town.

Ask Queen Beeyotch

Dear Queen Beeyotchular:

Girl, how am I gonna get my bidonk into college? All these admissions peeps think I got time to be writing some 500-word essay on a "seminar moment" in my life. Point-blank, period: I can't be attending no seminars unless they're www. I'm addicted to Facebook, and I love me some Farmville.

Hooked on Facebook

Dear Hooked on Phonics:

Wow. I assume you meant "seminal moment"—a life-changer. Here's some life-changing advice for you: Fumigate Farmville, bid farewell to Facebook, and grow the F up. Getting into a good college/university is going to require a lot more "E" for effort. I just received an early acceptance letter from Brown University–that's in Rhode Island, not Cabo San Lucas—and I didn't grab their attention by sending their office of admissions a round of virtual peachtinis.

Seems to me these essays are mostly the same for every university. They want you to demonstrate character growth, how you handled a situation that forced you outside your comfort zone to see the bigger picture. I wrote mine on learning forgiveness, and believe me, the lesson wasn't easy. For instance, I still haven't pardoned you for asking this ridonk question, and I doubt I ever will.
QUEEN BEEYOTCH

Trying to avoid a repeat Holiday Shores catfight, I broke the news to Abby on Mom's behalf. Before she lost her marbles, I showed her the Forgiveness Contract (à la Ms. Lambert's GG contract) I'd composed on a McDonald's napkin in Mom's car after we'd finished walking. In it, I'd laid out the terms of Mom's reconciliation with the Baker Siblings:

1. The only concession stand you'll be working at is Abby and Jay's Junk Food Trolley. Meaning, Abby would like a Diet Coke from McDonald's whenever possible; Jay will have what you're having sans cheese. We'll start you out at zero dollars an hour, no benefits.
2. Remember that SuperNanny software you tried to install on Jay's MacBook? She's decided to take up residence inside your flat . . . screen monitor. Cheerio!
3. You're single. Own it. For six months. If you meet

someone beforehand, this candidate must undergo a strenuous vetting process that may include a fingerprint background check for prior d-baggerly conduct. Also, he must keep standard business hours and shave regularly.

I pointed to Mom's signature at the bottom, and Abby nodded her head in approval. Then I pulled the deal-sealer from my pocket—the ring box containing Mom's gift—and handed it over to her.

"What the hell is this?" Abby asked, opening the box.

"Every truce begins with Jay," I said.

Upon learning of Abby's acceptance into Brown, Mom had her jeweler solder my great-grandmother's wedding ring to my grandma's. The diamonds were reset to make the bauble look less like a binding contract, more like an impressive piece of bling.

"Abby B., will you accept this peace offering?"

"Our grandmothers' rings?" she said, ignoring my bad Chris Harrison imitation and putting the ring on—a perfect fit.

"Yep. Mom said to congratulate you on getting into Brown. She loves you . . . just don't marry Eric."

"She didn't say the part about Eric," Abby said, wiping her eyes.

"Nope, that was me."

"But these rings mean so much to her."

"So do you," I said simply.

Not quite ready to type the words herself, later on my sister had me text the following to Mom: "Thanks . . . I love you."

I Bribed Gossip Girl, and She Told Me the Following

They don't call me the Anderson Cooper of Blogger for nothing. All in the name of intrepid journalism, again I braved the dangerous foreign territory known as the Indian Lake Rollarena in search of Gossip Girl. The unofficial bouncer, a suspicious-looking Japanese man who refers to himself as Benny Hana, informed me she was inside, and I found her doing an impressive series of triple toe loops underneath the disco ball.

Upon seeing the twenty in my hand, she stopped spinning, nearly threw up the row of Soft Batch cookies she'd eaten earlier, and then spouted the following into my tape recorder:

"Spotted: Freshman Blogfather skating away with his Doubles Partner du Jour to his school's secret exit door. I guess they needed to 'practice their routine.' I was not trying to judge the technical merit of Blogfather's flying moose knuckle, but one onlooker who couldn't stop staring came away with this artistic impression: 'Okay, so, Cher Horowitz from *Clueless* is my idol and I hooked them back up. Their mutual cluelessness is adorable, and that's what makes them Baldwin/Betty perfection, you know?' Gossip Girl says, As if. XOXO plus some trans fat."

Leave it to Gossip Girl to blow up the Blogfather's blogspot. That duplicitous minx claims to be allergic to love potion #9 (made with high-fructose corn syrup and the tender tears of Scott Hamilton), but don't be deceived. Gossip Girl craves kinship, too, and I know for a fact that she's programmed "Chippewa" into her GPS. Stay tuned for details on which ILHS student she's got her Garmin on.

Caroline's mom had been sober for thirty days and counting—her dad was etching marks into a tree outside their house with his army knife. With our mothers under control, C-line and I were two peeps in an iPod, our music library extending by the day. As for "Cher Horowitz," well, Cameo Appearance Parnell had bigger frosh to fry....

When I told Mike that our parents hadn't hooked up (the second time), he was grateful. Poor dude was hanging on to his baby for dear life; in his defense, though, he had the munchies all the time now. Per my recommendation, he'd nabbed himself his first girlfriend: Chippewa native Jennifer, who'd broken up with Greg when she found him searching her underwear drawer for her Vicky's Secret stash (it was there).

Maple Lane Tennis Tournament Results

"You're going to get shellacked in the final."
—Lon Richardson, my girlfriend's father

Game, set, match, he was right. I squeezed past my first two opponents in three sets, but a freak of nature creamed my powerpuff balls for winners in the final. No, it wasn't my girlfriend, Caroline Richardson, who beat me. She dominated the girls' draw, also carrying me to victory in the mixed doubles event. I'll be keeping the trophy (on the pillow beside me). Were there really twenty of you in attendance? That's what we tennis players call a "packed clubhouse." Lame, quip, natch.

Special thanks to Alice "A-List" Hudson, who's been kind enough to cart my ass to and from Maple Lane tennis lessons lately, not to mention carbo-load me to the brim. Your spaghetti is anything but D-List, A-List.

Classroom Suicide Watch with Cameo Appearance Parnell (and Special Guest Star Ms. Lambert)

Cameo: Hey, y'all! It's Cameo Appearance Parnell. Pleasure to make your acquaintance.

Jay: Since Cameo Appearance Parnell is so in tune with what's making ILHS students *Les*

Misérables, I've decided to make her a permanent addition to *Edumacation*'s CSW section.

CAMEO: It's true. I nearly stuck my head into the air-conditioning vent the other day during Mr. Microscope's "Single-Celled Organisms" lecture/trigger puller. Howevs, don't mistake Jay's laziness for altruisticness. Is that a word?

JAY: Altruism.

CAMEO: Yeah, that too. See how down-to-earth I am? Any-yoo-hoo, it's my first week on the job, and I landed an interview with ILHS government teacher Ms. Lambert. Welcome to "Classroom Suicide Watch," Ms. Lambert.

MS. LAMBERT: Thank you, apple dumpling. It's great to be here, finally, special-guest-star status and all. I feel like Heather Locklear on *Melrose Place.* Ha!

JAY: We like our guests to feel comfortable. All about klass here at *Edumacation.*

MS. LAMBERT: Sure you are.

CAMEO: So let's clear the proverbial desk with our microminis, like Amanda Woodward would, and ask some questions!

JAY: I have to get one out of the way first, Cam. When are you going to admit that you stole "Ha!" from *Alf,* Ms. Lambert?

MS. LAMBERT: When you admit to watching *Alf.* Oh, wait, you just did. Ha!

CAMEO: Let's focus on the issues, you two. As you know, Ms. Lambert, we here at *Edumacation* have been receiving reports of startlingly low brain wave activity during certain classes. Ahem, someone was telling me about the Lunesta moth landing on his desk during your Sandra Day O'Snoozer Supreme Court lecture.

JAY: I nearly caught it.

CAMEO: Do you have anything you'd like to say to Jay and the other O'Snoozer survivors, Ms. Lambert?

MS. LAMBERT: Of course, sunshine. I'd like to tell them to get over it.

JAY: Thanks, but it's been difficult.

MS. LAMBERT: You ingrates have no idea how much time and effort goes into keeping your attention. . . .

(Pointless argument ensues.)

CAMEO: We're back. Ms. Lambert, I would like to take a moment to thank you publicly for helping me take first prize in last week's "Search for a Star" competition.

MS. LAMBERT: No problem. It was touch-and-go there for a minute, but once we made it past your "Baby One More Time" ballad idea, we really found our groove.

CAMEO: Yes, we slowed down Jack Johnson's "Better Together" instead. To paraphrase Randy Jackson, I blew it out the box, y'all.

Ms. Lambert: By the by, Jay, we've dubbed our partnership "The La-La Sisterhood" in honor of you and your bad puns.

Jay: In that case, who wears the traveling pants in your relationship?

Ms. Lambert: See what I mean, America?

Cameo: So brutal.

Jay: I guess they're keeping it a Divine Secret.

Ms. Lambert: I'm living proof—for now—that "Suicide Watch" should include teachers' experiences as well.

Jay: (Laughing) Cameo, you won an all-expenses-paid trip to this summer's *American Idol* tryouts, and you get to bring a guest. Who will you be taking with you?

Cameo: Errrrrrr . . .

Jay: Oh, c'mon. You gave birth to my sea monkeys.

Ms. Lambert: I have a lovely song in mind: Patty Griffin's "Forgiveness." Cameo is making the right decision in taking yours truly—especially since I have her in class next semester.

Jay: Any plans to improve the O'Snoozer lecture by then?

Ms. Lambert: Must you always have the last word?

Jay: . . . Yes.

Suggested Playah-list

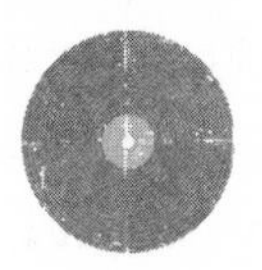

TRACK 1: "Superstar," The Carpenters

TRACK 2: "What's Love Got to Do with It," Tina Turner

TRACK 3: "Love Child," Diana Ross and the Supremes

TRACK 4: "We Will Rock You," Queen

TRACK 5: "Hoochie Mama," 2 Live Crew

TRACK 6: "Smells Like Teen Spirit," Nirvana

TRACK 7: "You're So Vain," Carly Simon

TRACK 8: "A Case of You," Joni Mitchell

TRACK 9: "I Kissed a Girl," Katy Perry

TRACK 10: "Let It Be," The Beatles

TRACK 11: "The Winner Takes It All," ABBA

TRACK 12: "Just Like a Pill," P!nk

TRACK 13: "Since U Been Gone," Kelly Clarkson

TRACK 14: "Landslide," Fleetwood Mac

TRACK 15: "Muskrat Love" and "Love Will Keep Us Together," Captain & Tennille

TRACK 16: "Bitter Sweet Symphony," The Verve

TRACK 17: "Reunited," Peaches & Herb

TRACK 18: "Ode to My Family," The Cranberries

TRACK 19: "Give Me One Reason," Tracy Chapman

TRACK 20: "I Just Called to Say I Love You," Stevie Wonder

TRACK 21: "Ice, Ice, Baby," Vanilla Ice

TRACK 22: "A Change Is Gonna Come," Sam Cooke

TRACK 23: "This Year's Love," David Gray

TRACK 24: "Cry Me a River," Justin Timberlake

TRACK 25: "Baby Got Back," Sir Mix-A-Lot

TRACK 26: "Rain," Patty Griffin

TRACK 27: "Dick in a Box" (featuring Justin Timberlake), The Lonely Island

TRACK 28: "Days Like This," Van Morrison

TRACK 29: "Apologize," OneRepublic

TRACK 30: "LoveGame," Lady Gaga

TRACK 31: "Every Rose Has Its Thorn," Poison

TRACK 32: "Sweet Home Alabama," Lynyrd Skynyrd

TRACK 33: "American Girls," Counting Crows

TRACK 34: "Viva la Vida," Coldplay

TRACK 35: "Family Affair," Mary J. Blige

TRACK 36: "Girl You Know It's True," Milli Vanilli

TRACK 37: "Sitting, Waiting, Wishing," Jack Johnson

TRACK 38: "Heads Carolina, Tails California," Jo Dee Messina

TRACK 39: "I'm Like a Bird," Nelly Furtado

TRACK 40: "Home," Daughtry

TRACK 41: "Heaven Knows I'm Miserable Now," The Smiths

TRACK 42: "Always Be My Baby," Mariah Carey

BONUS TRACKS:

"The Tracks of My Tears," Smokey Robinson & the Miracles; "Speeding Cars," Imogen Heap; "Forgiveness," Patty Griffin; "Roses and Cigarettes," Ray LaMontagne; "Arms," Seabear; "The Heart of Life," John Mayer; "Just Friends," Gavin DeGraw; "Waiting for My Real Life to Begin," Colin Hay; "That Year," Brandi Carlile; "Sweet Caroline," Neil Diamond; "Tony," Patty Griffin